"You definit[...] [...] probably to blam[...] [...] pening here," the [...]

Phoebe didn't confirm Fiona's assumption. She also didn't mention that she could see the smoky streams and hazes swirling around the rice scattered on the floor.

"Is the rice supposed to keep them away?" Phoebe asked.

"No, it distracts them," Fiona said. "I don't know why, but playful spirits feel compelled to count every grain."

That seemed to be working as intended, Phoebe realized. "Can you see them?" she asked Fiona. Ghosts were usually invisible to adult humans unless they wanted to be seen.

"No, I just sense them." Fiona tossed more rice behind her. A filmy strand spiraled down from the ceiling and circled the grains. "Counting rice will keep them from harassing your guests until they return to the otherworld at dawn."

"That's an interesting theory." Phoebe wasn't ready to admit that she knew ghosts existed or that visiting dead relatives accounted for most of Fiona's previous EMF readings. The ghost hunter's agenda was still unknown, and they couldn't risk having the Manor outed as a haunted house. Paige contemplated her next move carefully.

"Let's go find my sisters."

Charmed®

Published by Simon & Schuster

TRICKERY TREAT

TRICKERY TREAT

An original novel by Diana G. Gallagher

Based on the hit TV series created by

Constance M. Burge

SIMON SPOTLIGHT ENTERTAINMENT
New York   London   Toronto   Sydney

S|S|E

SIMON SPOTLIGHT ENTERTAINMENT
An imprint of Simon & Schuster Children's Publishing Division
1230 Avenue of the Americas, New York, New York 10020
® and © 2008 Spelling Television Inc. A CBS Company. All Rights Reserved.
All rights reserved, including the right of reproduction in whole or in part in any form.
SIMON SPOTLIGHT ENTERTAINMENT and related logo are trademarks of Simon & Schuster, Inc.
Manufactured in the United States of America
First Edition 10 9 8 7 6 5 4 3 2 1
Library of Congress Control Number 2007928094
ISBN-13: 978-1-4169-3670-1
ISBN-10: 1-4169-3670-X

For my daughter Chelsea,
the best Halloween treat ever!

Chapter One

Piper Halliwell tossed an old leather suitcase to Leo and swatted at a thick mat of cobwebs. The cardboard box was right where she and Grams had stashed it twenty years ago. Red crayon writing, scrawled in Piper's nine-year-old hand, was faded but still legible: *Halliwell Halloween Dec.* She had run out of room to finish the word "decorations."

"Bingo!" Piper pulled the carton away from the attic wall. Dust billowed off the box when she ripped off the sealing tape and folded back the flaps.

As his wife carefully unpacked, Leo fanned the cloud away from his face to peer inside. "It looks like every Halloween project you and your sisters ever made is in here."

"Every single project we made *is* in there," Piper said. "Grams unpacked this box every October when we were kids, and every year we added new things when she repacked it. This

1

year, we'll start saving things Wyatt and Chris make."

Piper glanced at their two children. Toddler Chris sat in his playpen, happily punching buttons on a pop-up toy. Wyatt was on his stomach, coloring in a new Halloween coloring book.

Leo held up a jack-o'-lantern made of stapled orange construction paper stuffed with cotton. The green paper stem and black facial features were still glued in place.

"Phoebe made that in first grade," Piper explained.

Wyatt jumped up and ran over. "Can I show Chris?" He held up his hand. A few months shy of four, he took being a big brother seriously.

"Okay, but don't let him hold it." Piper smiled at the mischievous toddler in the playpen whose inquisitive nature tended to result in his taking things apart. "Aunt Phoebe would be very sad if he ripped it."

"I'll be careful." Wyatt took the paper pumpkin from his father.

Leo reached back into the box and pulled out a twelve-inch wooden skeleton. The dangling bones were connected with brown twine. Wyatt dashed back to take the skeleton, too.

Piper picked up a porcelain doll named Hannah. The doll had a pretty face and ringlets of dark, shiny hair, but it was obvious that she wasn't dressed in her original clothes. Hannah wore a witch's costume, complete with a white lace pinafore, a broomstick, and a conical hat. Grams had made the doll clothes, insisting that witches were not old and ugly with warts and green skin. At the time, Piper had thought her grandmother was being silly. Now, as one of the three most powerful witches in the world, she, too, bristled at the commercial stereotype.

Almost everything in the Manor reminded Piper of Grams. She had not yet turned five when her mother died, and Grams had raised her and her sisters. A strong-willed woman with a warm, generous heart, Grams had preserved the family when the girls were children. Her death had brought them back together as young adults. The loving blood-bond of sisters reinforced the magical heritage of the Warren witch line that bound them as the Charmed Ones.

"How long has it been since you used this stuff?" Leo asked.

"Since we were teenagers," Piper reminisced. "Grams stopped decorating when we stopped trick-or-treating to go to parties."

Leo smiled. "Well, this year you'll have trick-or-treating *and* a party."

"Yea!" Wyatt cheered, then returned to his game of peek-a-boo with his brother and Phoebe's stuffed pumpkin. "Boo!"

Chris shook the wooden skeleton and laughed.

"I am so glad we found this box." Piper rubbed a smudge off the doll's face.

"Remembering where you put it helped," Leo said. "Everything your family ever owned is in this house . . . somewhere."

Piper stole a glance at the piles of treasures and junk in the cluttered attic. The open space in the center had grown smaller as the family had grown larger, and more boxes and keepsakes were added.

"Not everything," Piper objected. "Just things that are magical or have sentimental value. And stuff we thought we might need again."

"Like I said, everything." Leo ducked when Piper playfully lobbed a crocheted pumpkin at him.

"The Halliwells have exquisite taste," Piper said, grinning. "We collected a lot of good stuff over the years."

"Over a *hundred* years," Leo said.

Piper nodded. The Victorian Manor had been rebuilt after the San Francisco earthquake damaged the original house in April 1906. The Spiritual Nexus was located at 1329 Prescott Street, and the family *had* to stay on the site. The concentration of power in the Nexus had the capacity to be good or evil, depending on the nature of the magic in proximity. The Halliwell home had kept it grounded in good until the Charmed Ones destroyed it, an extreme but necessary measure to prevent the evil Zankou from taking control.

A whole century of Halliwell history, Piper

thought. Most twenty-first-century American families had become modern nomads, moving as often as whim and employment opportunities dictated. She and Leo would never abandon the Manor. A brief sojourn into their distant future proved that for a fact.

"What's in here?" Leo tried the suitcase clasps, but they were locked. He shoved the case into the space vacated by the decorations box. "No key. Never mind."

"You're a wise man, Leo Wyatt," Piper said. The attic contained hazards as well as treasures. Some of the magical booby traps were too easy to set off by accident. Three years ago, a "Return to Owner" spell on a pair of Grams' red go-go boots had sent Paige back to 1967. After being married with the same ring six times, Grams had cursed it to remind her not to marry again. Piper gave the ring to Cole to give to Phoebe as an engagement ring, and it turned her sister into a compulsive homemaker.

"That's for sure," Leo agreed. "With a house full of people tomorrow night, we don't need any witchy weirdness running amuck."

"Don't even think it," Piper said.

Opening the Manor to entertain friends and neighbors was something Piper had always wanted to do. And now, for the first time in eight years, since her powers had been restored after Grams' death, her life was settled and safe enough to throw a Halloween holiday bash.

Piper shuddered. "I'd rather not have to explain green goblin rashes or an epidemic of fairy fungus fever."

"Or something worse," Leo said.

"The Woogy Man has left the premises." Piper meant to calm Leo's anxiety. Instead, the reference to the Shadow Demon—vanquished when they destroyed the Nexus and blew up the basement—heightened his concern.

"Yes, but the Manor will never be a danger-free zone," Leo said.

Piper followed Leo's gaze to the scorched wall near the door. The wood was blackened where the wall had taken a fireball hit meant for her and her sisters. Christy Jenkins, Billie's long-lost older sister, had been raised by the Triad to kill the Charmed Ones. She had hurled the flaming orb a split second before Paige orbed them out. Leo kept procrastinating about fixing the damage. Piper suspected he wanted to keep the burn to remind her she wasn't invincible.

"It's been five months since we defeated the Ultimate Power and vanquished the Triad," Piper said.

Christy was dead, and Billie was now their ally. An above-average white witch, she was still their promising protégé and a good friend. The three regenerating demons had been the last evil force with the power to imperil the sisters' Charmed existence. The Triad wouldn't be coming back, and it would be years before the next generation of demons was strong enough to challenge them.

"Demons aren't the only enemy." Leo's gaze darted to the attic door, then to the window. "There are other forces."

"Nothing we can't handle," Piper countered. "The Power of Three may lead ordinary lives now, but we didn't retire. Besides, all the big bad guys are history."

Piper wished Leo would lighten up. Things had changed dramatically now that all the major demonic powers were gone. Every now and then, the Charmed Ones still had to fight something evil to save an Innocent, but Piper no longer lived in constant dread of being attacked or losing Leo. She wanted to savor every minute of the practically normal life she had finally achieved. Leo, however, seemed stuck in a perpetual state of wariness and fear.

"Lesser demons also caused a lot of trouble in the past," Leo said. "A scratch turned you into a Wendigo."

"That was years ago!" Piper protested.

Leo pressed. "Phoebe's broken heart made her susceptible to the banshee, and Paige was bitten by a vampire. All of you almost ended up as six-inch ceramic figurines."

"And your point?" Piper asked, annoyed.

"Other evil entities can be just as deadly as demons," Leo said. "And there are still plenty of them out there. Even if you and your sisters aren't the primary targets, the Powers-That-Be will keep connecting you to Innocents that need supernatural help."

"Of course, but I'm not going to look for trouble, Leo. I *like* being happy and relaxed."

"And *I* like happy Piper," Leo said. "But the bad guys will have an advantage if you let down your guard. So don't get too relaxed, okay?"

"I won't," Piper said with a sincere nod. "Promise."

Piper had anguished about Leo so much over the past few years that she couldn't be mad at him for worrying about her. *Even if it isn't necessary.* Her Charmed instincts and abilities were too ingrained to forsake her when she needed them.

"This punkin' wants to be real," Wyatt said. "Like the wood boy in the book."

"Boo-kah!" Chris squealed and rattled the skeleton.

"No magic, Wyatt," Piper reminded her powerful and precocious son.

"Good call," Leo whispered. "A Pinocchio pumpkin would be harder to explain than gooey green skin lesions."

"What time do we have to be at the Manor tomorrow?" Coop walked up behind Phoebe, slipped his arms around her waist, and nuzzled her neck.

Phoebe turned off the kitchen faucet and

faked an irritated scowl. "I can't wash apples and make out at the same time."

"Is choosing a problem?" Coop frowned, pretending to be puzzled.

"Only under dire circumstances," Phoebe replied, struggling to look serious. She was too happy to be convincing.

She had the perfect job, writing "Ask Phoebe," an advice column at the *Bay Mirror*. Her boss, Elise Rothman, also gave her as much latitude and time off as she needed whenever she needed—with no questions asked—for Charmed business. And now, after one failed marriage, to Cole—who had led a triple life as himself, the demon Belthazor, and the Source—and countless other relationships that had ended badly for more typical reasons, she had finally found true love with a Cupid.

"That's odd." Coop squinted furtively around the apartment. "I don't detect anything on my demon, danger, and dire circumstance meter."

"Then it obviously isn't calibrated for Piper on the warpath," Phoebe joked. "I promised I'd have my to-do list finished on time. Would *you* want to be responsible for wrecking the fabulous neighborhood open house she's been planning her whole life?"

"Absolutely not." Coop nibbled Phoebe's ear.

Phoebe sighed, enjoying his tender touch for a moment. It was not, however, a stolen or fleeting moment of bliss. Thanks to grown-up Wyatt and Chris, she *knew* they would be together "as one" for the rest of their lives. She would have millions of passionate, loving moments to cherish.

"Do you really think a few dirty apples could ruin everything?" Coop asked.

"Dirty apples would be a disaster." Phoebe gently pushed him away. "Everything has to be perfect.

"Nothing is perfect," Coop said, "except you and me."

"I know." Phoebe smiled, but she resisted the temptation to melt into his embrace. "And Piper knows she can't throw a party without something going wrong. But I don't want that something to be *my* fault."

"Touché!" Coop released her with a disappointed sigh.

"Here." Phoebe whipped the dish towel off her shoulder and pointed to the apples in the sink. "Make yourself useful, and dry."

"They're just going to get wet again," Coop said with endearing male logic.

"These aren't the bobbing apples," Phoebe explained. "They're going in the fruit basket on the buffet table."

"Oh." Coop took the dish towel.

"Put them in this for now." Phoebe reached for a metal colander on the counter. When she touched it, the familiar effects of a premonition jolted her.

. . . *Coop stormed around the Manor dining room*

in a violent rage. He was seething with anger, screaming vile threats, throwing things . . . at some-one beyond her perception . . . someone unseen and unknown. . . .

Me? Phoebe wondered as she snapped back to the present.

Coop's attention was on the apples in the sink. He didn't know she had slipped into a trance, and that was a relief. Phoebe hadn't had many premonitions since the Charmed Ones had dealt with the Triad, and of them, none had packed such a significant emotional punch. This premonition left her more shaken than she wanted Coop to know.

But not because Phoebe suddenly suspected that her kind and gentle soul mate was hiding a Jekyll-and-Hyde personality.

The disturbing premonition had the opposite effect. She and Coop were so perfectly matched, she couldn't help but feel a little unnerved now and then. It was like waiting for your new car to get a scratch. But rather than support her nervousness, the premonition made it clear that Phoebe's trust in Coop was sound and unshakable.

Coop couldn't be responsible for the vicious attack. An unknown evil had to be involved.

"How's that?" Coop held up a newly cleaned apple, grabbing Phoebe's attention.

"Perfect," Phoebe said, holding out the colander. "One down and twenty-three to go."

While she emptied the dishwasher, Phoebe

considered the fragment of the future she had glimpsed. The details were fuzzy, but she had seen a jack-o'-lantern in the dining room.

As a Charmed One, Phoebe's thoughts quickly turned to protection. The events she foresaw could be averted if proper steps were taken. However, avoiding the Manor on Halloween wasn't an option. Piper was counting on her and Coop to keep Wyatt and Chris occupied during the day and to help out with the party.

"What time do we have to be at the Manor in the morning?" Coop asked again.

"Around nine," Phoebe said as she picked up a towel to help Coop with the drying. "I thought it would be fun to take Wyatt and Chris to the Halloween Carnival."

"What's Leo doing?" Coop asked.

"Stringing lights on the Manor with Henry," Phoebe explained. "And we have to pick up our costumes by four."

"It's not too late to change our minds," Coop said. "We could still go as Antony and Cleopatra."

"No way." Phoebe playfully snapped him with her towel. "Cleopatra lost her love and died!"

"Good point." Grabbing the end of Phoebe's towel, Coop pulled her toward him and kissed her.

Despite the potential threat, Phoebe decided not to tell Coop or anyone else about the vision until she had more information. She didn't want to spoil the family's Halloween if it wasn't necessary.

And it might not be necessary.

Wyatt loved carved pumpkins so much, Piper usually kept the jack-o'-lanterns until they started to rot. Coop's rampage might not take place until days after the party was over.

Paige sat on a bench outside the mall entrance and dialed the Parole office.

"Mitchell." Henry's tone was clipped and all business.

"Mitchell's wife," Paige replied, matching her husband's no-nonsense demeanor. "What are you doing for lunch, mister?"

"That depends on where we're having lunch," Henry said.

Paige smiled at his softening manner. She hated to miss a romantic afternoon tryst with her wonderful husband, but Piper's party had priority. "I'm at the mall."

Henry sighed. "Well, the daily special at Luigi's isn't exactly what I had in mind, but I'll suffer through it."

"You love Luigi's lasagna!" Paige exclaimed.

"Not as much as I love you." He paused, then asked, "What are you doing at the mall?"

"Halloween shopping," Paige said.

Long before Paige knew she was a witch, she had loved Halloween. As kids, her Halliwell half-sisters hadn't known they were witches either. After they were grown and had emerged as the Power of Three, they tried to keep their observance as low-key as possible—for good reason. Once they had dressed up for a costume party at P3 and were whisked through a time portal back to 1670. They saved Melinda, the founding matriarch of the Warren witch line, from being raised by an evil witch. However, as a result of the adventure, the Halliwell sisters had curtailed their Halloween enthusiasm until Wyatt was born.

"I bought lights and talking tombstones and creepy plastic ghouls at the discount store," Paige explained. "But I'd like to find something special for Piper's party."

"A World's Best Witch trophy?" Henry suggested.

"I was going for gift-shop-cute-and-spooky, but I'll keep that in mind," Paige said. "I'll know what I want when I see it."

"I have an appointment in ten minutes," Henry said. "I'll meet you at Luigi's in an hour."

"See you there." Paige folded her phone with a wry smile. She had finally adjusted to Henry's rigid work schedule, but it hadn't been easy.

The duties and demands of being a Charmed One had taken over her life. She had given up her career as a social worker to study witchcraft, and then she had worked temp jobs to have flexibility. More often than not, the jobs brought her into contact with Innocents that needed her magical expertise.

On the plus side, Paige's life had settled into a relatively uneventful routine since the Charmed Ones had vanquished the Triad. After five years of relentless doom and destruction, she was content with her new, less hectic and less intense existence as the three basic Ws: wife, witch, and Whitelighter. Her current charge's powers hadn't manifested yet, and she could watch over the girl from afar. Refining her cooking skills, taking care of her home and husband, and helping Leo prepare Magic School for its reopening kept Paige as busy as she wanted to be.

There was only one glitch in her wonderful life: a lingering guilt about O'Brien and his leprechaun friends. After they had agreed to help the Charmed Ones defeat the Ultimate Power, she had betrayed them.

Paige slipped her cell phone into her bag and entered the mall. She hoped her quest for the perfect present would help her repress the painful memory again.

Christy Jenkins and her evil mentor, Dumain, were pawns in the Triad's plot to kill the Charmed Ones. To turn the Charmed Ones' allies against them, Christy and Dumain had unleashed a horde of assassin demons on the kingdom of mythical creatures. Paige had been under Christy's hex spell when O'Brien begged for help. It wasn't her fault that she ignored the

desperate leprechaun, but that didn't alleviate
her sense of responsibility.

The blood of every magical being slaughtered
in that assassin demon attack was on her hands.

Chapter Two

Piper flipped on the oven light and bent over to look through the window in the door. Her famous apple cinnamon cookies were just beginning to turn golden brown and were the first of several varieties she planned to bake before midafternoon. If she got everything else done on time, she wanted to make a traditional Irish barnbrack cake.

"Semitraditional," Piper muttered as she listened to the timer tick off the seconds. She had small metal trinkets to bake into the cake as the Irish recipe instructed, but she would not bake in the customary piece of rag. According to legend, the cloth brought bad luck to the person who found it.

"Chris wants a cookie," Wyatt said from the doorway.

"In a few minutes. They're not done yet." Piper brushed a strand of hair off her face and frowned at her son's bare legs. "Where're your pants?"

Wyatt shrugged. "Don't know."

"We can't find them." Leo walked in holding Chris.

"He has a drawer full of pants!" Piper picked up the oven mitts and counted to ten. She had promised herself she wouldn't spend all day being a nervous wreck, driving everyone else crazy. It was just a party. The world wouldn't end if her chocolate crème cake roll wasn't properly chilled or if she didn't have time to dust under the knickknacks. Still, Leo was entirely capable of dressing the boys without her help.

"He wants his camouflage sweats," Leo said.

"My soldier pants are lost." Wyatt rested his elbows on a chair and dropped his chin in his hands.

Wyatt looked so unhappy, Piper's annoyance burst like a bubble.

"I looked everywhere," Leo said. "They're not under his bed or in the laundry."

Piper knew that. Wyatt had outgrown the faded sweatpants, and she had given them to the local fire station for the annual Firemen's Charity Clothes Drive. Eventually, she'd have to tell Wyatt the truth, but not today. He'd forget all about the missing pants when Aunt Phoebe and Uncle Coop arrived to take both boys to the Halloween Carnival at the Community Center. Piper didn't want to miss the fun, but she had to concentrate on party prep.

"Those pants are too small for you, sweetheart," Piper said softly. "Wear your black ones. That's a good Halloween color."

"Okay." Wyatt sighed and left, shoulders slumped and feet dragging.

"Have you heard from Henry and Paige?" Leo put Chris in the high chair and strapped him in.

"They're on their way." Piper pulled the tray of cookies out of the oven. They smelled delicious.

"Kah-ki!" Chris held out his hands. One of the hot cookies orbed off the cookie sheet.

"No!" Piper froze the cookie in midair before it reached Chris and burned his hand.

"Kah-ki!" Chris started to cry.

"Hot!" Leo caught the cookie when it fell and gingerly flipped it from one hand to the other. "Ow. Hot!"

"Hut." Chris sniffled and stuck out his lower lip.

"Yes, very hut." Leo broke the cookie in half and blew on it. When it was cool enough to eat, he put the two pieces on Chris's tray. "Do you need anything else before I get the ladder, Piper?"

"Are all the pumpkins carved?"

"Yesterday," Leo said. "Just as you asked."

"I'm missing a box of decorations, but Paige can look for it." Piper slipped a second sheet of apple cinnamon cookies into the oven and set the timer. "She's going to finish cleaning while I cook. So as long as you and Henry don't fall off the roof, we're good."

"Knock on wood." Leo rapped on the kitchen table, then kissed Piper on the cheek. "You really shouldn't press your luck."

"I know," Piper agreed with a tight, satisfied smile. "But now *you'll* be extra careful, won't you?"

"Actually, yes." Leo kissed her again, grabbed a cookie, and turned to leave.

"Don't forget to spray the bales of straw and corn stalks for bugs!" Piper called after him.

"Kah-ki hut?" Chris asked.

"Cookie cool now." Smiling, Piper scooped another cookie off the sheet and gave it to Chris. It didn't matter if the party went off exactly as planned. Her family was healthy and happy, and they were going to have a wonderful Halloween. "With no witchy weirdness."

"Wicky." Chris orbed another cookie into his chubby hand.

"Wow!" Phoebe exclaimed as she and Wyatt entered the Community Center. "This is a Halloween wonderland!"

The building was jammed with food tables, craft booths, and homemade carnival games. Every nook and cranny was festooned with corn stalks, orange and black streamers, jack-o'-lanterns, skeletons, and other traditional decorations. Spooky sound effects blared from loudspeakers by the haunted house in the back corner. Adults dressed like zombies, ghouls, witches, and ghosts prowled the aisles, mingling with parents and wide-eyed children.

"These people go all out, don't they?" Coop observed as he carried Chris into the center.

"Boo!" Chris waved at a large ghost dangling from the ceiling.

"That's right, Chris!" Coop grinned. "It's a ghost."

"He calls all Halloween stuff 'boo'," Wyatt said.

"Just remember the cookies, and don't let him orb," Phoebe warned in a whisper. She and Coop were still getting used to being married. They planned to have children someday, but proper parenting wasn't a pressing issue at the moment. Making sure Chris didn't vanish in a sparkling swirl of light was. "Just give him whatever he wants."

"Uncle Coop has it under control," Coop assured her.

"Ride!" Chris jiggled in Coop's arms. His baby gaze was fastened on a coin-operated car ride.

Phoebe gave Coop a fistful of quarters. "He rides the airplane at the supermarket five or six times before he'll quit without screaming."

"Thanks for the tip," Coop said.

"What do you want to do first?" Phoebe asked Wyatt.

"I don't know," Wyatt said.

"Of course you don't," Phoebe said. "There are so many neat things to choose from, I can't decide, either. So let's just walk, and you tell me when to stop."

"Don't forget your trick-or-treat bag." A man by the door handed Wyatt a plastic bag decorated with black cats and pumpkins.

Wyatt asked for two treats at every booth, one for him and one for Chris.

"You are such a good brother, Wyatt," Phoebe said. "We'll have to find something extra special for you."

"Fireman!" Wyatt pulled Phoebe toward the local fire station's make-a-costume display. Greg, one of Piper's old flames and still a family friend, was on duty.

"Hey, Wyatt!" Greg squatted down to talk. "How you doing, buddy? Want to make a costume?"

Wyatt shook his head.

"He's going as a pirate this year," Phoebe said.

"We might have something you can use." Greg waved his hand over the costume supplies strewn across the tables and stuffed in boxes. "Feel free to look."

"I want that!" Wyatt climbed on a chair and pulled a camouflage jacket out of a box. It was several sizes too big.

"You won't grow into that for years," Phoebe said.

"It's like my soldier pants," Wyatt said. "But they're lost."

Greg's good-natured smile faded. He pulled Phoebe aside and spoke softly. "Piper donated a pair of kid's camouflage sweatpants to the clothes drive."

"She gave away Wyatt's favorite pants?" Phoebe was surprised and appalled. When she was twelve, Grams threw away her favorite Bon Jovi t-shirt because it had a few holes in it. It had felt like a betrayal, and she had never forgotten.

"She said he outgrew them," Greg explained. "I thought they'd make a good kid costume so I brought them here."

"Well, thank goodness for that," Phoebe said, relieved. "Can I have them back, please?"

Greg looked pained. "Another little guy took them first thing this morning. Sorry."

Wyatt pretended he couldn't hear what Greg and Aunt Phoebe were saying. He wasn't very big, but he was pretty smart. He was also very good. If Aunt Phoebe told him not to use magic, he wouldn't use magic.

So he couldn't let Aunt Phoebe know that he knew what happened to his favorite pants. Then she wouldn't know that he was going to use magic to get them back.

Wyatt turned away from the adults. He couldn't use simple wish or picture magic because he didn't know the boy's name or where he lived. So he had to cast a saying spell like Mommy used. He had never tried that before, but he knew the words had to sound alike.

Wyatt closed his eyes and pictured the pants in his mind. He thought up words that fit and crossed his fingers.

> *Soldier pants,*
> *Green and black,*
> *Come back!*

Wyatt smiled. That would work. Now he could have fun.

Paige stood in the middle of the attic. Piper couldn't find the plastic skeleton they always hung in the front hall, or the HAPPY HALLOWEEN banner that stretched across the dining room window. She had sent Paige upstairs to find the missing decorations.

"Except I don't know where to look," Paige muttered. Piper had remembered where she put a box of handmade decorations two decades ago, but no one knew what had happened to the box they packed last year. "So I'll just have to pick a spot and start."

Working from the inside back toward the walls, Paige began a systematic search. She didn't cast a locator spell on the off chance that making her task easier might be considered personal gain. The last thing Piper needed at her party was magic gone awry.

The monotony of rummaging through stacks of magazines, boxes of clothes, and miscellaneous magical paraphernalia was broken by snatches of conversation between Leo and Henry as they stomped around the roof.

"How many kids do you want?" Leo asked.

"Six," Henry answered.

Six! Startled, Paige lost her balance. She stumbled off the step stool, toppling a stack of cartons and winter quilts. She didn't fall, but two boxes broke open when they hit the floor.

"Seriously?" Leo laughed. "We'll have to build a new wing at Magic School!"

"Will they all have powers?" Henry asked.

"They'll all be Whitelighters," Leo said. "It's probably fifty-fifty on the witch part."

Henry was quiet for a few seconds. "Then three is all I can handle."

Ditto that. Paige moved to the window to join the banter, but the two men were already going down the ladder. As she turned around, she spotted her shillelagh lying on the floor. A leprechaun named Riley had given it to her as a thank-you gift after she broke a wicked witch's spell that had made him tall.

Paige's brown eyes filled with tears of grief and regret as she closed her fingers over the knotted wood. Before the assassin demons attacked the magical realm, killing O'Brien's friend Liam and many other mystical beings, she had complained about being the liaison between the Charmed Ones and the leprechauns. She hadn't known how much she would miss them.

Paige sank onto the red Victorian settee, clutching the shillelagh to her chest. "I wish there was a way to fix things with the little guys."

O'Brien and two other leprechauns arrived in the attic via the Rainbow Road.

"O'Brien!" Paige gasped, surprised by the unexpected visit. "What are you doing here?"

"You're wantin' to make things right with us, and we're here to bargain." O'Brien gestured toward his companions. "We might be makin' a deal, if you can convince Connor and young Grady you're as sincerely sorry as you sound."

Paige looked the leprechaun in the eye. "I've never been sorrier about anything."

Grady, younger and shorter than O'Brien and Connor, with a round face and rosy cheeks, stepped closer and peered into Paige's eyes. "I believe her."

Paige leaned forward. "You'll forgive me?"

"When our luck runs out and our gold is gone," Connor growled. The elderly leprechaun was slightly stooped, with a wrinkled face and a cranky frown.

"Meaning never." Paige sighed.

"Liam was a gentle soul and a dear friend." Connor's bitter tone and accusing gaze stung.

"Aye, and I've been listenin' to you moan and groan about wantin' to tell him that yourself for months, Connor," O'Brien said. "That's why we came, don't forget. To beg the favor Paige owes."

"What favor?" Paige asked with a trace of suspicion. Leprechauns were industrious, crafty, and true to their word, but they weren't prone to playing mean pranks. However, it was Halloween. The usual rules of behavior might not apply.

"We want to see Liam," Connor answered.

"You want me to summon him?" Paige didn't immediately reject the idea. She couldn't erase the assassin demon tragedy from history or her heart, but the pain would be more bearable if Liam didn't blame her.

"In a manner of speaking." O'Brien smiled. "We want to celebrate Samhain with those of us who died helping the Charmed Ones."

"*Sow-en?*" Paige asked, repeating the Celtic word.

"The end of summer," Connor said impatiently.

"A grand festival to mark the harvest and the beginning of winter," O'Brien added, "as the Irish have always done."

"I very much want to bid Seamus and Liam a proper farewell," Grady said.

"And Marty," Connor added.

"You didn't know Martin personally," O'Brien told Paige.

But she had known Seamus Fitzpatrick. Paige met the leprechaun when she cast a luck spell to recoup some of the family's out-of-pocket Charmed expenses. Seamus asked the witches to stop a reptilian demon that was stealing leprechaun luck. Saleel killed Seamus before a meteor crushed Saleel.

"May they rest in peace." Connor removed his tam and bowed his head.

"After the party," Grady said.

"You know about Piper's party?" The wariness Paige felt intensified.

"Aye," O'Brien said. "A party's just what we're needin' to honor our fallen comrades, as the dead were honored at Samhain in olden times."

"When the barrier between this world and the realm of the dead became passable," Connor said, "and the spirits of the departed walked among the living."

"For real." In Paige's studies of the occult, she had learned that the degree of belief could enhance or diminish the power of certain rituals, potions, or spells. Without the conviction of an entire population, the barrier that had opened between worlds thousands of years ago remained closed in modern times.

Unless magic is applied, Paige mused.

"Samhain was Seamus and Liam's favorite festival." Grady grinned. "Seamus always lit the bonfire, and Liam carved the most intricate turnips."

"Turnips?" Paige asked, puzzled.

"Our ancestors carved turnips as protection from evil spirits," O'Brien explained. "It's a tradition."

"Like jack-o'-lanterns," Paige said.

"Actually, that's another story," O'Brien said, "but I'll be saving it to tell later, at the party."

Paige cleared her throat. "About the party—"

Connor scowled. "You wouldn't be trying to say we're not welcome, now, would you?"

Paige hesitated, caught in a quandary. Piper wouldn't appreciate the addition of mischievous little men to the guest list, but how could she deny the leprechauns' request? Christy and Dumain had ordered the assassin demons to murder magical Innocents to weaken the Charmed Ones, so the deaths were indirectly their fault.

"I wouldn't think of it," Paige said, abruptly shifting gears. The leprechauns' need for closure with their friends seemed as important as her need to make amends. The Charmed Ones had summoned Grams, Patty, and other spirits without harm on many occasions. "But you have to promise me something."

"What?" Marty asked suspiciously.

"Don't tell anyone that you're leprechauns," Paige said. "If anyone asks, just say you're actors. And don't cause any trouble I won't be able to explain."

O'Brien smiled. "As you wish."

Paige had to take him at his word. "I'll cast the spell just before sundown."

"Until then, lassie." O'Brien executed a sweeping bow as the Rainbow Express whisked him away.

Paige sighed, hoping she wouldn't regret her decision yet knowing she couldn't pass up a chance to heal the rift with the leprechauns. Piper would understand that.

Wouldn't she?

Chapter Three

"Paige!" Piper slapped a young leprechaun's hand as he reached toward a platter on the dining room table. "You stop that this instant," she told him.

The little man pouted. "I'm hungry."

"Nobody touches this buffet until the real guests arrive." Piper raised her wooden spoon to fend off the six uninvited munchkins. She had spent two hours using cookie cutters to make the deviled ham finger sandwiches in Halloween shapes. They were off limits until the party started.

"Don't snap at Grady." Seamus glared at her. "You're supposed to feed us!"

"That's what people do on Samhain, Piper," Liam said. "They put out food and drinks so the spirits won't be makin' trouble."

"If I had known you were coming, I would have made more," Piper countered, annoyed. Paige should have warned her. "Aren't you guys dead?"

"They are, and that's a fact," O'Brien said. "There'll be many a ghost about tonight, but not all will be harmless or as easy to please as Liam, Seamus, and Marty. Some are as foul and vicious in death as they was livin'."

"Some are worse," the old leprechaun said gravely.

"But most are just a nuisance," O'Brien finished.

A ribbon of cold air suddenly twined around Piper's legs and curled up her arm. The icy sting stilled the breath in her throat, and the spoon flipped out of her hand.

"See!" O'Brien exclaimed.

The leprechauns shivered, one after the other, as though the cold current were weaving a serpentine course in and around them. Ice crystals formed on Marty's beard, then melted so quickly, Piper wasn't sure she had seen them.

"Paige!" Piper called again.

"What?" Paige hurried down the stairs into the dining room. She looked stunning as Maid Marian. A gold cord belted the crimson outer gown she wore over a beige homespun dress. Her matching head cloth was held in place by a gold headband.

"There are leprechauns and cold invisible thingies in the dining room!" Piper exclaimed. "Do you know why?"

"Well . . ." Paige winced. "O'Brien wanted to

spend Halloween with his dead friends, so I summoned them."

"Grady and Connor aren't dead," O'Brien clarified.

"Yet!" Fuming, Piper picked up the spoon. "What were you thinking, Paige?"

"That it's our fault Seamus and Liam and Marty died, so it was the least I could do," Paige explained.

"A little hospitality wouldn't hurt either," the grumpy Connor said.

"Here." Piper tossed him a bag of candy corn. She had plenty left over from last year, when Leo had overstocked. Nobody liked candy corn. *Except leprechauns, apparently,* she realized when they all reached out.

Grady caught the bag. "Thank you."

Seamus tipped his hat, and the six little men filed into the living room.

"The cold air is probably just a draft." Paige rubbed her arms. "This *is* an old house."

"Or Leo and Henry left a window open somewhere," Piper said. The temperature had been colder than usual the past few days. The brisk October air, full moon on the wane, and cloudless sky made for a perfect Halloween night.

"I'll check." Paige headed into the kitchen.

"Thanks!" Piper continued arranging iced sugar cookies on a black plastic tray, wishing she hadn't gotten upset. Paige thought she had betrayed the leprechauns, and the guilt was eroding her happiness and self-esteem. Piper could deal with a few magical short guys if it would restore her half-sister's confidence and peace of mind.

"We have leprechauns in the living room." Leo paused in the hall doorway. He looked dashing in a colonial commodore's uniform, complete with epaulets, three-cornered hat, and sword.

"Be glad they're not trolls." Piper picked up the empty cookie tin. "Who won the sword fight?"

"I did!" Wyatt ran in, swinging a toy pirate sword. In boots, pants, and tunic with a red overcoat, belt, and plumed hat, he closely resembled the pirate captain in his favorite storybook. He wouldn't wear the black wig and gold earring. The wig itched, and the earring pinched.

"You look fantastic!" Piper nodded with approval. She was glad he had gotten over the large camouflage jacket he had brought home from the Community Center. She honestly hadn't realized how attached he was to his "missing" pants. Hopefully, she would be able to find a new pair that fit.

"Shouldn't you get dressed, Piper?" Leo looked at his pocket watch.

"As soon as Paige comes back to answer the door," Piper said. Her colonial lady's outfit complimented Leo's commodore costume. It had also been a good choice for someone on a tight schedule. The elegant gown zipped and came with a white powdered wig. She only needed ten minutes to change.

Wyatt tugged on Leo's coat. "Can we go trick-or-treating now?"

"As soon as Grandpa and Chris are ready," Leo said.

Piper smiled. An absentee dad for most of his daughters' teenaged years, Victor had come back into their lives after Grams died, to protect them from magic. Over time, he had learned to accept their Charmed destiny, and they had learned to love and depend on him.

"Let's go," Victor said as he hurried down the stairs. He wore a black sweatshirt decorated with white skeleton ribs and a button by his belly. "Chris wants candy."

"Candy!" Chris was an adorable ghost. Piper had cut and hemmed a circular hole in a white pillowcase for his face. The toddler pushed the button on Victor's sweatshirt and squealed when a spooky voice laughed.

"Let me!" Wyatt pushed the button next.

Victor grinned. "I knew I'd be the hit of the trick-or-treat crowd."

Piper gave the boys plastic candy bags and watched them troop down the front stairs. "Don't let them eat too much!"

"I can't hear you!" her father shouted back.

Smiling, Piper leaned against the doorjamb. Her family was finally able to relax and enjoy the simple pleasures others took for granted. It felt good.

"May I have a food bag?" Grady asked.

"Sorry, I'm all out." Piper frowned as the leprechauns marched out the front door. "Where are you going?"

"To have a bit o' fun." Seamus grinned.

"And to stuff our pockets with sweets." Connor yanked Grady across the porch. "You don't need a bag. Use your hat if there's more than you can eat or carry."

"I'm hoping for a good leg o' mutton." Marty rubbed his stomach. "With a pint o' cider to wash it down."

"Mince cakes." Liam licked his lips.

"And woe to them what isn't generous." Seamus waved as he started down the steps.

"Wait! You can't go trick-or-treating." Piper moved to stop them. O'Brien pulled her back.

"Let them go," O'Brien said. "You'll have nothing but trickery trouble if you ruin their fun."

"They're expecting mutton and cider," Piper said. "Our neighbors give candy to *children*. What happens if someone insults them and sends them away empty-handed?"

"Then it's a trick or two they'll be playing, no doubt." Seeing her look of horror, O'Brien added, "Harmless tricks, to be sure."

Piper hesitated. It was unrealistic to think she could dissuade the leprechauns from celebrating

Samhain in their own way. They might rattle a few nerves here and there, but they weren't dangerous. Besides, her neighbors and friends would be arriving soon. She still had to get into her costume, and the Manor's first trick-or-treater was headed up the stone steps.

O'Brien welcomed a small boy and his mother. "And who might you be?"

"An army guy." The boy wore a helmet, drab green T-shirt, and camouflage sweatpants that looked like Wyatt's. "What are you?"

"A leprechaun, don't you know." O'Brien bowed.

"Where'd you get such a cool costume?" Piper asked the boy. The Bartlett family lived on the next block, and Tony went to preschool with Wyatt.

"In my closet," Tony said, shifting from one foot to the other.

"We got the pants from the make-a-costume booth at the Community Center," his mother added. Margo wasn't in costume.

"Really?" Piper couldn't be positive that the sweatpants were Wyatt's. Even if they were, it would be too embarrassing and tacky to ask for them back. Wyatt would have to be satisfied with a new pair.

"I thought he'd want to trick-or-treat on our street first," Margo explained, "but he wanted to come straight here. Are we too early for the party?"

"No," Piper fibbed. "I just have to change—"

"Where's my candy?" Tony asked, bouncing. His mother leaned over and whispered in his ear. "Oh, yeah." The boy sighed in exasperation. "Trick-or-treat."

"Right this way, laddie." O'Brien ducked back inside to retrieve the candy bowl.

"Is he allergic to anything?" Piper always separated the candy into three bowls: chocolate, sugar-free, and chocolate with nuts.

"No." Margo inspected the display at the front of the house. Leo had created a creepy scene with hay bales, corn stalks, pumpkins, a scarecrow, and an assortment of black cats, ravens, spiders, and rats Paige had found at the discount store. Camp lanterns bathed the area in muted light and shadow. "Your house decorations are fantastic!"

"Thank you, I'll tell my husband." Piper was just as impressed. Leo and Henry had worked all day on their macabre masterpiece.

Both sides of the stone steps had been transformed into a graveyard with lights, sound effects, amusing tombstones, coffins, and miscellaneous creatures of the night. The house was adorned with hundreds of orange lights. All the strings worked, and neither man had broken or sprained anything putting them up.

"Hey!" O'Brien yelled. "Come back here now!"

Piper and Margo exchanged a startled look.

They dashed inside just as O'Brien disappeared into the living room, chasing Tony.

The boy had been so fidgety, Piper thought he needed to use the bathroom.

"Where's Wyatt?" Tony shouted. "Wyatt!"

"Tony! Come back here," Margo ordered.

"He's headed for the kitchen!" O'Brien yelled.

Piper and Margo split up. Tony's mom followed O'Brien through the sunroom. Piper ran into the dining room to protect her refreshments. The Halloween spread of canapés, sandwiches, doughnuts, popcorn balls, cookies, and cakes had taken days to prepare. One small berserk boy could demolish the buffet in an instant.

"Wyatt!" Tony shouted in the kitchen.

"Hey!" Paige exclaimed. "Watch out!"

Pots and pans clattered, and O'Brien yelped, "Ouch!"

Piper winced. The boy's rowdy rampage through the Manor was bizarre. Tony was quiet and shy at preschool, and he never misbehaved on his playdates with Wyatt.

"Stop this right now, Tony Bartlett," Margo demanded.

"Wyatt! Where are you?" Tony burst out of the kitchen into the dining room and made a hard right turn.

Piper stretched her arms out to protect the table as Tony raced by. Another gust of icy air stung her face. She glanced at the fireplace, wondering if the draft were coming through the open flu. She made a mental note to close it—after they captured Tony.

"Wyatt isn't up there!" Piper yelled as the boy bounded up the stairs.

Tony spun around on the landing and ran back down.

Piper grabbed the flower arrangement off the hall table so it wouldn't be broken. The container, a ceramic pumpkin flanked by a cute ghost and black cat, held autumn mums, mini sunflowers, daisies, oak leaves, and wheat sprigs. Paige had given her the centerpiece.

Margo snagged Tony's shirt as he ran by.

"Let me go!" Tony struggled.

"Calm down or I'm taking you home," Margo said. "No trick-or-treating and no party. It's up to you."

Tony stopped fighting.

"I am so sorry, Piper," Margo apologized. "He's never done anything like this before."

"He's just excited," Piper said. "Wyatt couldn't wait to go trick-or-treating. He left with his dad and grandfather just before you got here."

Tony yanked free and ran for the door. "C'mon, Mom!"

"I guess he wants candy after all." Margo dashed after her son. "Tony! Wait!"

"What was that all about?" Paige walked in holding a brownie.

"A Halloween sugar high, maybe? I'm not

sure." Piper eyed the brownie with a scowl. "Did you take that off the table?"

"And risk getting whacked with a spoon?" Paige rolled her eyes. "No."

Piper glanced up the stairs as Henry started down.

Henry wore a shirt with billowing sleeves, a green tunic, a sheath of arrows, and a distinctly merry expression. He touched the brim of his feathered cap. "Good evening, ladies."

Paige frowned when Henry hit the landing. "You're not wearing the tights!"

"Not on pain of death." With a sheepish grin, Henry glanced down at his jeans and scuffed work boots, then at his wife. "It's half a Robin Hood, or no Robin Hood."

"Whatever makes you happy." Paige held out her hand and curtseyed when Henry kissed it. As she straightened, she frowned again. "Is that smoke?"

"Where?" O'Brien stood in the dining room doorway, dabbing powdered sugar off his mouth with a napkin.

Piper was too shocked to scold O'Brien for raiding the goodies. Her heart clutched at the thought of fire.

"Over there." Paige pointed toward the living room doors.

"A wisp, was it?" O'Brien asked as Henry hurried to investigate. "Or a whisper?"

"A wisp or a whisper of what?" Piper asked.

"Small spirits," O'Brien explained. "Beings without guile: wee tots, pets, and the like. They may have scooted in with Liam and all."

Henry stepped back into the hall. "I don't see smoke or a fire, and I don't smell anything burning."

"Well, that's good." Paige nodded as though to convince herself, then looked at Piper. "Right?"

"The house isn't burning down," Piper said. "That's good. An infestation of spiritual wisps and whispers? Probably not so good."

O'Brien waved away her concern. "Except for puttin' a chill in the air, they're mostly a playful lot. Nothing to worry about."

"I don't have time to worry. I have to change." Piper headed for the stairs. "You three—hold the doors!"

Chapter Four

"Have fun!" Phoebe smiled as a tiny ballerina and a fuzzy bear scurried back to the sidewalk and their dad. She had definitely gotten the better part of the deal when she chose door detail. The house was full of guests, and her sisters had to constantly restock the buffet. It was just after nine, and the stream of trick-or-treaters had dwindled to a trickle.

Time to party! As Phoebe closed the door, someone yanked on her shirt and she stumbled. "Coop!"

Phoebe glanced back, but Coop wasn't behind her. No one was in the hall.

The tug wasn't the first oddity Phoebe had encountered since arriving at the Manor that evening. She had seen gossamer tendrils in the bathroom mirror and heard heavy breathing in the pantry. The strange incidents had to be connected to O'Brien's ghostly wisps. They didn't seem dangerous or connected to her premonition, but she ramped up her alert status another notch.

"Happy trails to you . . ." Singing softly to settle her nerves, Phoebe added what was left of the sugar-free and plain chocolate candies to the bowl of chocolate with nuts.

This was Coop's first Halloween as a member of the Halliwell family. After much deliberation, they had decided to come as Roy Rogers, a 1940s singing movie cowboy, and Dale Evans. Roy and Dale had fallen in love, married, and stayed true to each other their entire lives. "Happy Trails" was the signature song of their 1950s western TV show.

". . . till we meet a-gain." Leaving the full bowl of candy by the door, Phoebe picked up the empty bowls and moved toward the kitchen.

A shriek slashed through the din of conversation and laughter. Everyone fell silent. The ominous strains of gothic music and spooky sound effects playing throughout the house sustained the suspense. The effect was broken when Piper flew out of the kitchen.

"What was that?" Piper barreled across the hall into the living room.

Phoebe followed her sister through the crowd to the sunroom. To their mutual relief, there was no freaky emergency. A little girl had soaked her face, hair, and princess costume bobbing for apples.

Wyatt, the neighborhood children, O'Brien,

and assorted parents were gathered around the apple tub. Leo had placed it on a plastic drop cloth to protect the floor. Victor sat in the rocker, bouncing Chris on his knee. Having exchanged his ghost costume for comfy pumpkin pajamas, Chris was fascinated with the laugh button on his grandfather's sweatshirt.

"Here you go." Leo pulled a towel off the stack behind him and held it out.

"Someone pushed me!" Nancy sobbed.

"Nobody pushed you." Nancy's mother wrapped the towel around the wet girl's shoulders. "You just slipped."

"The wee lass should get a prize," O'Brien said. "It's not everyone gets a dookin' by a ghost."

"There's no such thing as ghosts." Abbey Cork had just turned thirteen, and she was less gullible than the younger kids.

"There are too." Eight years old and extremely bright, Vanessa Moreno was convinced.

"Nancy didn't catch an apple," ten-year-old Ryan pointed out.

"Aye." O'Brien nodded and handed the sniffling girl a party-favor bag. "All the more reason to give her a prize."

"Can I have one?" Ryan asked.

"Bite an apple first, Ryan," Abbey teased. She was in charge of Vanessa and her brother until both sets of parents returned from working a charity event. The kids didn't want to miss the party, and the sisters were keeping watch over all of them.

"How many favor bags do we have?" Phoebe asked Piper.

"More than enough for everyone." Piper pushed a wisp of hair back under her colonial wig. The cascade of white ringlets accented a fake beauty mark and made Piper's brown eyes appear darker than usual. The blue and gold brocade gown masked her hostess anxiety with a false façade of hauteur. "How's the candy holding out?"

"Fine, but if we need more"—Phoebe glanced at the two huge bags of candy Wyatt and Chris had brought home—"we can always raid the kids' stash."

"Or use last year's candy corn." Piper took the two empty bowls from Phoebe. "Don't let O'Brien get too carried away with the creepy tall tales. We don't need an epidemic of nightmares breaking out in the neighborhood."

Phoebe jumped when a woman in the living room screeched. "Now what?"

"Something's crawling up my leg!" A woman jumped on a chair and stamped her feet. "It feels like a snake!"

Across the room, Coop and Henry stopped talking. Phoebe met Coop's questioning gaze, shook her head, and shrugged. Then she smiled. She couldn't help it. Coop even looked gorgeous in his corny cowboy outfit: white hat, red-and-white checkered shirt, jeans, western boots, and a bandana tied around his neck. Her costume was almost the same except she wore a skirt, her fringed shirt was blue, and she didn't have spurs.

"Stand still, Sybil!" The panicked woman's husband patted down her pants. "I don't feel anything."

"You don't?" Sybil shook her leg, then frowned. "I don't feel it now either."

"Something just like that happened to me a few minutes ago," another woman said. "I could have sworn someone kissed my neck, but there wasn't anyone there. It was an exquisitely chilling feeling."

"Maybe the Manor's haunted," Fran Winslow said. Dressed as a 1920s flapper, she nervously looped her feather boa around her neck.

Piper quickly countered that idea. "Not haunted: special effects."

"Cold-air machines," Leo added, playing along to end the discussion. "By the upstairs vents."

"The fizzing ice cubes are great." A man wearing an ordinary sports coat and a Sherlock Holmes hat turned to Piper. "How did you make them fizzle into crystals like that? Dry ice?"

"Trade secret," Piper said, smiling tightly.

"Good one," another guest agreed.

"First I've heard of it," Phoebe whispered to

Piper. She was not comforted knowing that other people had witnessed bizarre phenomena too. "What's *really* up with the ice and the phantom kisses?"

"Piper!" Paige called from the kitchen. "I think the fondue is done!"

"I'll explain later." Piper turned to leave. "Just keep an eye on things out here, okay?"

"Sure." Phoebe didn't mind. Listening to the leprechaun's stories gave her an excuse to watch Coop. The details in her premonition were a blur, and she didn't know if he was wearing a red-and-white checked shirt when he became a raving maniac. She didn't sense any tension or suppressed hostility in him now, but he could lose it at any moment.

"Why do we carve pumpkins?" a boy asked.

"We didn't have pumpkins in Ireland way back when I—" O'Brien caught himself. "Back in olden times. People carved turnips to keep the evil spirits away."

Vanessa giggled. "How could a turnip do that?"

O'Brien lowered his voice. "On account of they was carved to look meaner than the ghosts. A turnip can look right fierce with a candle stuck inside."

All the children leaned in to listen.

"Then why don't we use turnips?" Ryan asked.

Phoebe covered her mouth to stifle a laugh.

Listening to the kids made her more eager to start a family with Coop.

"Turnips are puny," O'Brien bellowed. "Big, fat pumpkins are much better!"

"Jack-o'-lanterns," Wyatt said.

"Aye," O'Brien said. "So called after Jack the blacksmith. He was a nasty man, a thief, and a mite too smart for his own good. Tricked the devil up a tree, Jack did, and made a magic sign on the trunk so that he couldn't get back down. And then—"

The kids tensed.

"—Jack made the devil promise not to let him into hell." O'Brien nodded and sat back.

"That sounds pretty smart to me," Abbey said.

"Remember, Jack was mean and a thief," O'Brien went on. "When he died, he couldn't go to heaven, and the devil wouldn't let him into hell. He was doomed to wander the Earth with nothing but a candle in a carved turnip to light his way. Jack's lantern."

"Oh!" Vanessa perked up. "I get it."

"Cool." Abbey smiled at Wyatt. "This is the best Halloween party I've ever been to."

This is the best Halloween party I've ever been to, Phoebe thought. The Halliwells were all happy and destined to live long, wonderful lives. The event foretold in her vision would just be a glitch in the bigger, brighter picture.

"You look deep in thought," Coop said, brushing Phoebe's neck with his lips.

"Just thinking about you," Phoebe quipped.

"Who wants to play Pin-the-Face-on-the Pumpkin?" Henry asked, as he came into the room with a box of game supplies. All the kids raised their hands. "Let's go, then. C'mon, Coop. You can help."

Vanessa hung back when the other kids followed Henry to the front hall. "Don't go away, Mr. O'Brien. I want to know more about ghosts."

"And why would a pretty little thing like you be wantin' to know about them?" O'Brien asked.

"Because I saw one in the window over there," Vanessa whispered to the leprechaun. Phoebe overheard and looked where the little girl pointed.

The haze on the windowpanes peeled off and flowed through a small crack in the ceiling.

Paige carried a fistful of fondue forks and a basket of French bread chunks to the dining room.

"Try this, O'Brien." Piper took a piece of bread and dipped it in the hot cheese mixture.

"I'd rather have a taste of that magnificent barnbrack cake." The leprechaun picked up a knife.

"Don't do that," Paige warned. She wasn't being ornery. Piper had wrapped metal coins, rings, and Halloween charms in paper and baked them in the traditional Irish fruitcake for the children.

"You can have a piece, O'Brien," Piper said, "as soon as the kids finish their game."

"You're a hard woman, Piper Halliwell." O'Brien sighed. "I'll probably get the slice with the bit o' rag, even though I've already had me share of bad luck this year."

"You're safe. I don't bake rags into my cakes." Fondue dripped off the bread Piper held in her fingers. She ate it.

"If you're not in dread of gettin' the tattered cloth, there's no relief when you don't," O'Brien complained.

By omitting the bad luck rag, Piper had sacrificed authenticity to protect the neighborhood children from the superstition. Paige approved.

"Traditions evolve for good reasons," O'Brien continued. He looked at Paige, then back to Piper. "You're looking much too fine and fancy this Samhain."

"Was that a compliment?" Piper asked, amused.

"A warning," O'Brien said. His gaze darted to Fran. "You best beware too, missy."

"Me?" Fran touched her chest and shifted her weight. The motion made the red fringe on her flapper dress shimmy.

"Apparently," Paige said.

Fran had been hovering by the table, eavesdropping. After her husband's sudden heart attack and death two years ago, she had developed an obsessive interest in the occult. For a while Fran insisted that Edward was haunting their home. Lately she had become determined to contact his spirit. A sucker for every New Age scam and trend that fed her hope, she was the type of person the sisters couldn't help and tried to avoid. Her beliefs and erratic behavior were driven by grief, not an evil entity that wished her harm.

"Beware of what?" Fran asked.

"Being taken away to the otherworld by ghosts," O'Brien said. "The druids wore masks and shrouded themselves in straw or white cloth to fool the evil spirits into thinkin' they were spirits too."

"Can they take me to Edward?" Fran asked.

"Our house isn't haunted, Fran," Piper said.

Not exactly, anyway, Paige thought as she picked up a stack of used paper cups and an empty plate. She headed toward the kitchen through the hall.

On edge since she had cast the summoning spell, Paige started to relax. O'Brien was having a great time stuffing himself with Piper's cuisine and making sure the children knew the origins of their Halloween customs. The other leprechauns were still trick-or-treating, without mishap, she hoped. The chilly antics of the stray spirit wisps were a huge hit with the guests, and the spooky "special" effects were a positive addition to the Halliwell mystique.

Paige paused by the stairs to watch the pumpkin game.

"Are you sure that's where you want it?" Henry asked Wyatt. The blindfolded boy stood with his arm stretched toward the paper pumpkin tacked to the wall.

"Higher," Ryan urged.

"Don't listen to him, Wyatt," Abbey said.

"And don't peek!" Coop admonished.

"I won't." Wyatt put the nose right between the pumpkin's eyes.

"That's pretty close, Wyatt." Henry used tape to secure the black triangle. "And you didn't even cheat."

Henry could handle six kids, Paige thought as she moved on to the kitchen. *But I'm not going to tell him that!*

Paige didn't expect to find Fran standing by the prep island, frowning at a silver platter. "Is something wrong?"

A moment passed before the entranced woman looked up.

"Did you see that?" Fran tentatively touched the silver dish with her fingertips. "I saw a woman's reflection in this plate. It was so clear. Then it just . . . dissolved."

"The lights can play tricks," Paige said. "You probably saw yourself for a second."

Fran huffed, offended. "Don't patronize me, Paige. I know what I saw. *You* just don't want to believe the evidence that's right in front of your eyes."

Paige played dumb. "Evidence of what?"

"That your house has a ghost." Fran forgot her indignation and spoke with earnest enthusiasm. "There are lots of haunted places in San Francisco."

Paige smiled weakly. She didn't know if Fran had seen one of O'Brien's wisps or if the woman's imagination had shifted into overdrive. Desperate to speak with her deceased husband, she had to be aware of the folklore regarding the passage of spirits between worlds on All Hallows' Eve. Most people would freak if confronted with a real ghost. Fran would be overjoyed.

That was the problem. Fran believed in the paranormal based on faith and desire, not evidence. They'd never be rid of her if she thought the Manor was a spiritual hot spot.

"You should contact this website called Hollow Hill," Fran suggested. "They track down—"

"Sorry, Fran," Paige interrupted. She had to get the woman back with the crowd, where she'd be less likely to have a ghostly encounter they couldn't explain. "We need more, uh . . . nuts!" The tin on the counter was the first thing that caught her eye. Paige grabbed it and shoved it at Fran. "Would you take this to the table? I have to check something."

"Check the lady in the silver platter." Fran turned on her heel, flipped her boa over her shoulder, and stomped out.

Paige sagged against the island. A crystal candy dish suddenly slid across the smooth surface. She caught it before it could fly off the edge.

"Be patient. There's plenty for everyone." Phoebe handed Abbey a plate with a sliver of barnbrack cake. "Chew carefully! Piper put metal things in this, and I don't want anyone to break a tooth."

"Did you ever see a ghost, Mr. O'Brien?" Vanessa asked.

"Not one as good as yours," O'Brien said. "But yes, I have. Would you like to hear about it?"

A man with short-cropped brown hair and glasses picked up a sandwich. He waited until O'Brien and Vanessa were gone before speaking. "Do you think it's a good idea to let that weird little man fill that child's head with such drivel?"

"Kids like scary stories," Leo said.

"Especially on Halloween." Phoebe didn't recognize the man. He was dressed in street clothes: slacks, a shirt, and a V-neck sweater-vest. "Are you new in the neighborhood?"

"Just visiting." The man grabbed a second sandwich and moved on, scanning the crowd.

Phoebe wondered which neighbor had brought him to the party.

Paige came up beside her. "Have you seen Fran?"

"I think she left." Phoebe glanced toward the hall. A few minutes ago Fran had tried to convince Piper to have someone verify the existence of a Manor ghost. "She was upset because Piper didn't want to list the house in some online haunted sites directory."

"I'm pretty sure she didn't leave," Paige said. "Fran's belief quotient is too high for her to buy our 'special effects' explanation. I think she saw a wisp and wants to prove it."

"Why?" Phoebe asked. "No one would believe her. The neighbors already think she's bonkers."

"Yes," Paige agreed, "but if she proves to herself that ghosts are real, she can justify the effort and expense of trying to contact Edward. Either way, for her sake and ours, we can't let her have another up close and personal sighting."

"Then we'd better find her." Phoebe handed the cake knife to Leo. "I'll look upstairs."

Small groups of people filled the hall. Phoebe paused to exchange pleasantries on her way to the stairs, then quickly excused herself. She didn't want to be rude, but haste was imperative to maintain the relative peace and quiet they had enjoyed the past few months. They could diffuse Fran's interest with patience, persistence, and a spell or two if necessary. Problem solved—as long as Fran didn't contact a more zealous and ambitious follower of the occult about her suspicions.

As Phoebe stepped onto the second floor, she realized it might already be too late to cork that bottle.

A woman with auburn hair wearing a hooded hunter-green cape was scattering rice around the hall.

Chapter Five

"Who are you, and what are you doing?" Phoebe asked, her tone stern.

The woman was not startled or unnerved at being caught where she didn't belong. Slipping the hood off her head, she smiled warmly and held out her hand. "Fiona Dunne."

An empath with acute powers of observation, Phoebe quickly assessed the intruder's character and intent.

The green cape covered a brown velour top and matching skirt hemmed at midcalf. The skirt overlapped high, soft leather boots. The muted colors and simple style indicated that Fiona Dunne did not dress to attract attention.

She doesn't need to, Phoebe thought. With a thick head of unruly auburn curls, high cheekbones, and freckles, Fiona had a wholesome, earthy beauty. Her green eyes shone with an intense intelligence and an impish zest for life. A self-assured woman, she was not a threat, at least not in an evil-demon-out-to-kill-you way.

But she was up to something.

Phoebe shook Fiona's hand. "Phoebe Halliwell. This is my family's home."

"I know," Fiona said. "I've been monitoring the EMF activity here for some time."

The blatant admission took Phoebe aback. "You've been spying on us?"

"No!" Fiona grinned, amused. "I look for and study obscure haunted sites. Mostly those no one else knows about. Some that the big-name pros don't want to bother with."

Phoebe blinked, the only outward sign of the alarms going off in her head. The Charmed Ones had dealt with demonic bounty hunters, witch hunters, and a gypsy hunter, but they had never crossed paths with a ghost hunter.

"The Manor isn't haunted," Phoebe said calmly.

"Yes, it is," Fiona said. "I've gotten some very intriguing readings over the past few years. The accumulated residual spiritual energy dropped rather suddenly about three and a half years ago—"

When the witch doctor cleansed the house of evil spiritual buildup. Phoebe kept her expression bland and the information to herself. The witch doctors wanted to eliminate the Charmed Ones, and the cleansing had been an excuse to acquire personal possessions for a hex.

"—but it's risen steadily again since then,"

Fiona went on. "I just hesitated to ask if I could investigate."

"Why?" Despite the need for caution, Phoebe was curious. The woman's unabashed honesty and willingness to answer questions was refreshing.

"There's always been an element of unrest and chaos surrounding this place," Fiona said. "I didn't want to add to it."

Honest, intuitive, and wise. Phoebe sensed a twinge of wariness and didn't ask if Fiona's résumé included psychic talents beyond detecting spirits.

"Then why are you here now?" Phoebe asked.

"A significant EMF upsurge and significantly less chaos," Fiona explained. "And since you're having an open house, I just walked in."

"What's EMF?" Although Phoebe and her sisters had encountered several ghosts since becoming witches, she wasn't familiar with ghost hunting terminology.

"Electromagnetic frequencies," Fiona explained. "Natural EMF radiation only happens near electrical activity or magnets. When there's a large EMF spike without a natural source, it's probably a ghost."

"How do you know there was an EMF spike?" Phoebe needed as much information as possible to determine how much of a problem Fiona presented. Kooks could usually be scared into giving up their occult pursuits. Fiona was not a kook, nor easily frightened.

"It registered on my meter." Fiona held out a device.

"That looks like a compass," Phoebe said.

"It is. An ordinary hiking compass." Edging closer, Fiona pointed to the dial. The needle was spinning wildly instead of pointing north. "You definitely have ghosts, and they're probably to blame for anything odd or inexplicable happening here," the caped woman continued.

Phoebe didn't confirm Fiona's assumption. She also didn't mention that she could see the smoky streams and hazes swirling around the rice scattered on the floor.

"Is the rice supposed to keep them away?" Phoebe asked.

"No, it distracts them," Fiona said. "I don't know why, but playful spirits feel compelled to count every grain."

That seemed to be working as intended, Phoebe realized. The wisps were drawn to the rice like a banshee to sorrow.

"Can you see them?" Phoebe asked. Witches and some small children could see spirits, but ghosts were usually invisible to adult humans unless they wanted to be seen.

"No, I just sense them." Fiona tossed more rice behind her. A filmy strand spiraled down from the ceiling and circled the grains. "Counting rice will keep them from harassing your guests until they return to the otherworld at dawn."

"That's an interesting theory." Phoebe wasn't ready to admit that she knew ghosts existed or that visiting dead relatives accounted for most of Fiona's previous EMF readings. The ghost hunter's agenda was still unknown, and they couldn't risk having the Manor outed as a haunted house. Paige contemplated her next move carefully.

"Let's go find my sisters."

The argument was beginning to escalate when Paige walked into the sunroom.

A man wearing glasses and a sweater-vest stared down at O'Brien. "The world has got enough problems without people like you spreading lies about voodoo dangers that don't exist."

"I do not lie." O'Brien huffed, his livid gaze boring into the stranger. "The world is full of fantastic things, harmless and horrible. They don't cease to be just because narrow-minded dimwits like *you* are too dense and blind to see them."

The lights suddenly dimmed, blinked off, and then flickered on again.

"There!" O'Brien exclaimed. "Who do you think did that?"

"Faulty wiring," the man said. "If you could prove what you're saying, you would."

"I'd be happy to oblige, but you don't have the good sense to accept what your eyes and ears tell ya!" O'Brien puffed out his chest. "A healthy dose of rotten luck might tame your ignorant tongue—"

"That's enough!" Paige glowered at O'Brien. Watching from the sidelines, she had hoped that good judgment and common sense would prevail. However, they were like stags locked in combat, and nothing less than an overwhelmingly stronger force could end the verbal duel.

"I appreciate your concern, Ms. Halliwell," the man said, "but this obnoxious runt—"

"It's Mrs. Mitchell," Paige said, cutting him off. "And Mr. O'Brien is a very good friend of the family. Who are you?"

"Ken Carson." He was neither embarrassed nor apologetic as he pulled out his wallet and handed Paige a card. "I'm in the psychology department at the university, and I've had quite a bit of experience debunking delusional nutcases."

"A hobby?" Paige struggled to hide her immediate dislike of the judgmental professor.

"Research," Ken replied. "I've been trying to discredit a fraudulent ghost hunter for years. I believe you may know her. Fiona Dunne?"

The name wasn't familiar.

"Paige!" Piper called. "Can I see you in the kitchen? Now, please!"

"Be right there!" Paige answered, then she

focused on the two men. "I'm sure neither of you want to spoil the party for everyone else. So why don't you just agree to disagree, okay?"

"Of course," Ken Carson said.

O'Brien harrumphed, but nodded.

"Thank you." Pocketing Ken's business card, Paige shot the leprechaun a warning look as she walked away. She and Piper had finished cooking an hour ago, so a summons to the kitchen meant trouble.

Piper wasn't waiting alone. A woman with auburn hair was sitting at the table beside Phoebe. A green cape was draped over the back of her chair.

"Have a seat, Paige." Piper poured hot water for tea into four cups.

"What's up?" Paige asked.

"This is Fiona Dunne," Phoebe said. "She's a ghost hunter."

"And according to her, the Manor is Grand Central Station for spirits tonight." Piper set the kettle back on the stove. A blast of cold air froze the steam escaping from the spout.

"That's an interesting effect," Fiona said. "I've never seen a spirit do that before. Their ability to manipulate the physical world is usually limited. I wonder if your paranormal powers have somehow enhanced their skills."

Paige gasped. "Our what?"

"I haven't said a word." Phoebe smiled tightly.

"Then where would she get such an absurd idea?" Piper's eyes flashed as she pulled up a chair.

"Fiona senses things," Phoebe explained. "Ghosts in particular."

"What do you think you know about us, Fiona?" Piper asked.

"Nothing specific." Fiona's composure didn't crack under Piper's bristling scrutiny. "But if I did, I would respect your privacy and never tell a soul."

Paige was inclined to believe her. For one thing, Phoebe was an empath. If Fiona couldn't be trusted, she'd know.

Piper wasn't as easy to convince. "You must want something."

"To satisfy my own curiosity," Fiona said. "Some people collect rocks. I collect ghosts. But I assure you, I do not want to expose the Manor's incredible spiritual properties."

"Assuming the Manor is haunted—" Paige was cut off by a rat-a-tat noise that sounded like large hailstones hitting the house. When the barrage ended, she continued as though nothing unusual had occurred. "Why would you keep it a secret?"

Given the general public's interest in ghosts and haunted houses, Paige thought it was a fair question. Unlike other mystical subjects, ghosts had popular acceptance and were accorded a measure of credence in the media.

"I don't want to be responsible for another tragedy," Fiona said.

"What tragedy?" Victor asked, stopping abruptly as he walked in.

"Just an, uh, unfortunate . . ." Phoebe paused, stumped for an explanation.

"All the plants died when Fiona took care of a friend's house," Paige said. "So she doesn't want any temp jobs that require taking care of potted pets."

"What can I say," Fiona added with a shrug. "I have a black thumb."

"I can't grow anything, either," Victor said. "Except daughters." He took a juice box from the fridge and left.

"You handled that well," Fiona said.

"We've had a lot of practice," Phoebe said. "I just didn't want to worry our father for no reason."

Piper asked the pertinent question again. "What tragedy?"

Fiona brushed a tangle of curls behind her ear and sipped tea before starting her story. "An old friend of mine found a ghost that was so active, the house could be easily documented as a haunted site. He went public with his findings and the location."

"And it turned into a three-ring circus," Piper said.

Fiona nodded. "The Benson family's life was turned upside down by amateur hunters and gawkers. When it got to be too much to take, they had the house torn down."

"That would be a hardship," Phoebe pointed out, "but hardly tragic in the classical sense."

"The story doesn't end there." Fiona spoke with the quiet confidence of someone who was knowledgeable and comfortable with her topic. "Ghosts are stuck in their own realities, planted, so to speak, within the specific parameters of whatever's keeping them from moving on—time, place, circumstances."

Or people. Paige recalled the ghosts of Leo's World War II soldier friends, Rick and Nathan Lang. They wrongly blamed Leo for their deaths at Guadalcanal and spent sixty years honing their corporeal powers just to kill him. They mortally wounded Piper instead, which was a fatal mistake. Piper was dead just long enough to vanquish the Lang brothers before Leo's healing powers brought her back.

"And it's always personal," Phoebe said. "I did some research on the ghost of Alcatraz once."

"Then you know that ghosts try to force everything to fit their reality," Fiona went on. "Electronic devices like radio and TV upset those that died in the nineteenth century, for instance. That's why so many strange incidents are associated with hauntings."

That was not what was happening tonight, but Paige didn't interrupt.

"When the Benson house was destroyed, the ghost lost the place that defined its reality." Fiona finished her tea and pushed the cup and saucer aside. "The spirit was so infuriated and traumatized, it developed incredible physical powers. Every attempt to use the land where the house once stood was disrupted. After a man died, the land was abandoned."

"That's terrible," Phoebe said. "Do things like that happen often?"

"No, thank goodness," Fiona said. "But I don't want to risk it. I have no desire to bring such misery to anyone—living or dead. No one will hear about your ghosts from me."

"The Manor isn't haunted," Piper insisted again.

"Are you finished with this plate, ma'am?" Coop asked in an exaggerated drawl. He had watched a couple of old westerns on cable so he could get into character. However, the cowboy chivalry encouraged the attractive neighbor to flirt.

"Yes, Coop, thank you." Eve batted her fake eyelashes. Wearing a blond wig and a white dress, she had come to the party as an old film star named Marilyn Monroe.

Phoebe called the dark spot on the woman's face a beauty mark. Coop dropped the paper plate into his trash bag and tried not to stare at it.

"You can have this, too." Eve smiled coyly and held out an empty paper cup.

As Coop reached to take it, he remembered Leo's warning and glanced around the room. Just over a year ago, Leo and the sisters had faked their own deaths so they could begin new, unencumbered lives. They had all assumed false identities using a spell that masked their true appearances. Eve had come on to Leo at a group playdate for their kids, while he was pretending to be a cousin called Louis. Blaming Leo for his wife's indiscretions, Carl had punched Leo in the jaw and sent him sprawling. Coop was relieved to see that Carl wasn't in the room. He did not want to fight.

"Just drop it in here." Coop opened the trash bag.

Suddenly, Eve's hand jerked. The cup sailed over her shoulder and hit the wall. "That's weird. I didn't mean to do that. My hand just went nuts."

"I've got a trick knee that buckles when I don't expect it," Coop said calmly. He couldn't explain that a mischievous spirit had tossed the cup. Eve wasn't curious or worried about the strange occurrence. She was focused on him.

"But you're so young!" Eve exclaimed.

"And my *wife* wants all this trash picked up pronto." Coop touched the brim of his hat and politely moved on. He took his time cleaning up near the window, where Wyatt was standing with Abbey and the Moreno kids.

"I'm sure it was hail," Abbey said, referring to the barrage that had hit the house a few minutes before. "Nobody could throw that many rocks at one time."

"A monster with a hundred arms could," Wyatt said.

"Yeah," Vanessa agreed, "but there aren't any monsters with a hundred arms."

"There aren't any monsters, period," Abbey said.

"Yes, there are," Ryan insisted. "The Loch Ness monster lives in Scotland. I saw it on TV."

"And some monsters can too have a hundred arms," Wyatt argued. "Want to see?"

An image of a gigantic centipede crushing the sofa flashed through Coop's mind. He blurted out, "No!"

Wyatt eyed Coop with youthful indignation. "I have a picture in my monster book, Uncle Coop."

"Yes, but . . ." Coop paused. With four pairs of curious child eyes staring at him, he needed a good excuse for his outburst. "But Mr. O'Brien looks kind of lonely sitting all by himself. He's probably got a dozen monster stories."

"At least," Vanessa said.

After the kids joined the leprechaun, Coop headed to the kitchen. He walked in just as Piper declared that the Manor wasn't haunted.

"But the ghosts that aren't here have stopped playing with the lights, throwing rocks, and changing the thermostat." Coop dropped the full trash bag by the back door.

"You're such a kidder." Phoebe cuffed his arm and shifted her gaze across the table.

Too late, Coop noticed the unfamiliar woman sitting at the table. He played along with Phoebe's ruse to cover his blunder. "A kidder and a kid at heart."

"Which is just one of the million things I love about you," Phoebe said.

Coop planted a kiss on her cheek and whispered "Oops" in her ear. Then he pulled a new trash bag from the box on the counter and left.

Paige smiled as Coop stopped to blow Phoebe another kiss from the door. The newlyweds were still in the honeymoon phase of their happily-ever-after romance.

"Seriously," Piper reiterated when Coop was gone, "we do not have a ghost."

"You don't have a *resident* ghost," Fiona said, "but I always detect residual energy when I take a reading here. There's an unusually enormous amount of activity right now." She held out a compass to prove her point.

Paige glanced at the fluctuating needle. That was curious, but not inexplicable. Then she remembered the man who had picked a fight with O'Brien. "A man in the sunroom mentioned your name. He said he's trying to prove you're a fraud."

"Ken Carson from the university?" Fiona asked.

"That's him. Glasses, sweater-vest, and a giant chip on his shoulder," Paige said.

"The jerk with the superior attitude?" Phoebe grimaced. "I thought he was here with friends."

Fiona sighed. "Ken is an associate professor. He's trying to make his academic mark by debunking my articles and theories. He follows me every Halloween."

"That explains why he was picking on O'Brien for telling ghost stories," Paige mused.

"Ken is a typical skeptic," Fiona said. "Arrogant and convinced he's right despite substantial evidence that supernatural phenomena are real. I don't know why he's singled me out."

Paige had an idea about that. Before they had destroyed all the powerful old-guard demons, every evil bad guy on the underworld leadership track had been out to kill the Charmed Ones. The sisters were the most powerful witches in the world. That made them a prominent target and the most valuable trophy.

"Are you the best at what you do?" Paige asked.

"I have a few impressive discoveries under my belt." Fiona took the tea bag Piper offered and held out her cup for more water. "As I said before, my reward is finding and authenticating obscure or previously unknown sites. I don't charge a fee for my investigations."

"That's a plus," Piper said. "With us, anyway."

"You really do believe, don't you?" Phoebe asked solemnly.

"Yes." Fiona nodded, then quickly added, "But I'm not a true believer. A lot of people fervently want ghosts to be real for all kinds of reasons. They find evidence where there isn't any, and they buy into all the pop culture myths."

"We know one of those," Paige quipped. "Fran would love to meet you, but she'd probably drive you crazy."

"Fran *is* crazy." Leo paused in the doorway and took off his three-cornered hat. He wiped his brow with his sleeve then used the hat to fan himself. "She swears she saw a ghost in the silver sugar bowl, and she's convinced the woman died when the house collapsed in the 1906 quake. Now she's trying to get the spirit to 'go into the light.'"

"And how is that going over?" Piper asked.

"About as well as you'd expect. Everybody thinks it's hilarious." Leo pulled at the ruffled jabot around his neck. "It's hot in here."

Beads of sweat formed on Paige's neck under her head cloth. She used the paper napkin under her teacup to dab at it. "Better check the thermostat again."

"Yeah, I'll do that." Leo replaced his hat. "I'm

concerned about Fran, Piper. She's making a fool of herself, and we can't exactly explain that she's more right than—" He stopped suddenly, his gaze zeroing in on Fiona.

"Leo, meet Fiona Dunne." Piper smiled. "Ghost hunter."

"We haven't voted on it yet," Paige said, "but I'm pretty sure she's the real deal, with no ulterior motives. Fiona just likes ghosts."

"Some of them," Fiona said. "I doubt there's a lost soul from 1906 haunting this house, though. You'd know about it. Lost souls are trapped by exceptionally powerful emotions after violent deaths. They're confused or want vengeance—"

"Or they're just stopped from crossing over by evil souls that make deals with demons . . ." Phoebe let the sentence trail off.

Paige didn't try to explain that Phoebe was once caught in a repeating loop with lost souls who died in a cabaret fire. They had all been freed when Count Roget was finally sent to his eternal punishment.

"The playful spirits in this house tonight have crossed over," Fiona said. "They're just visiting. Ghosts, on the other hand, can't or won't let go of their earthly bonds."

"Visiting from where?" Leo asked.

The streamers of black and orange crepe paper framing the doorway started flapping, as though whipped by a strong wind. The individ-

ual streamers on each side twined into cords and
encircled Leo's arms.

"What the—!" Leo's surprise was replaced by
alarm. "They're tightening . . . " He ripped at the
paper ropes, trying to break their hold.

Piper raised her hands and flicked her fingers. Everything in the kitchen froze except the
sisters and the streamers. The paper continued
to tighten.

"Why didn't the decorations freeze?" Paige
asked.

"Remember Frankie and Lulu?" Piper
scowled.

"How could I forget?" Phoebe shuddered.

Paige had been visiting her past when the
malicious spirits of the gangster lovers had
arrived through another ghost's time portal. After
taking over Phoebe and Cole's bodies, Frankie
and Lulu had robbed a jewelry store and a bridal
shop so they could get married. Clyde, the portal
ghost, captured them before they took their vows.

"I can't freeze ghosts," Piper said.

"But Elias Lundy's lightning strikes froze,"
Phoebe said, adding as she turned to Paige, "A
ghost we vanquished before we knew you."

"The bolts froze *after* they left his fingers,"
Piper said. "This ghost must be hands-on with
the streamers."

Paige glanced at the frozen ghost hunter.

Fiona looked as fascinated by Leo's predica-
ment as she was startled. They had done

everything but make a formal announcement
that they were witches. If Fiona didn't know
exactly who they were or what they could do,
she probably wouldn't be too surprised when
she found out in thirty seconds. Paige didn't
have time to get a consensus. She had to act
before Leo lost his lower arms.

The instant Piper unfroze the scene, Paige
called, "Coat!" She swept her arm across the
room, orbing Leo's long coat into the sink. The
streamers were still wound around the coat
sleeves.

"Thanks, Paige." Rubbing his arms to restore
the circulation, Leo staggered to a chair.

"You're welcome," Paige said.

"That's a lot more magic than I expected,"
Fiona said flatly.

"We're the real deal too," Phoebe said. "But
it's a secret, like sensing things. You understand."

"Perfectly," Fiona replied.

Phoebe's phrasing and Fiona's answer suggested that the ghost hunter had more psychic
ability than she wanted anyone to know. That
created an unspoken bond of trust.

Piper read between the lines as well and
relaxed. She looked at Leo. "What was the question?"

"Where did these visiting spirits come from?"

"Good question." Piper turned to Paige.

"What spell did you use when you invited O'Brien's dead friends to the open house?"

"The same summoning spell we always use," Paige said.

Fiona's eyes widened. "You opened the way for spirits to cross over on Halloween?"

"O'Brien wanted to celebrate Samhain with his friends one more time, and I sort of owed him," Paige said.

"The same man who tells stories?" Fiona asked.

"The same leprechaun," Paige specified. *In for a penny, in for a pound.* If something had gone haywire with her spell, every little detail was important. They might need Fiona's expertise to solve a ghost problem, so she had to know everything.

"We thought the wisps hitchhiked in from the otherworld with Liam, Seamus, and Marty," Leo said.

"They're the dead leprechauns that O'Brien, Connor, and Grady wanted to see," Paige explained.

Phoebe looked up sharply. "Where are they?"

"Trick-or-treating," Piper said.

Fiona gasped.

"It's not as bad as it sounds," Paige said, trying to reassure her. "Leprechauns can be cantankerous pests, but—"

"I'm not worried about the leprechauns,"

Fiona said. "But your spell to summon them may have opened a portal for other spirits."

Leo's head snapped toward Fiona. "If Paige lowered the barrier, we could be inundated with spirits that haven't been able to enter the world of the living for centuries."

"Why is that?" Piper asked. "Not that I'm complaining."

"Most people don't believe in ghosts anymore," Leo said, "except on Halloween. It's the one night a year when masses of people are more open to the existence of the supernatural."

"What are you saying?" Phoebe asked. "That Paige's spell got a belief boost?"

"It could be that simple." Leo shrugged. "The law of unintended consequences applies to magic, too."

"Is there quartz in the land under the Manor?" Fiona asked. "Quartz absorbs and retains magical energy. That could affect a spell."

"No quartz," Piper said.

"And no more Spiritual Nexus," Phoebe added. "Just plain old rock and dirt."

"Actually, it probably doesn't matter *why* Paige's spell opened the door between worlds," Phoebe said. "The playful spirits are busy counting rice."

Leo, Piper, and Paige looked askance at Phoebe.

"Fiona scattered rice in the upstairs hall," Phoebe explained. "The wisps will count it all night. Then, after they return to the otherworld with the leprechauns at dawn, the portal will close, with no serious harm done."

"We couldn't be that lucky," Leo said.

"You're not." Fiona pointed at the floor.

A line of large puddles shaped like footprints appeared as an invisible entity trudged across the room.

Chapter Six

Henry moved the apple-bobbing tub against the wall before someone tripped over it. Piper's party was a bigger success than she had hoped, and he didn't want a small flood or a sprained ankle to upset things.

"People sure are strange," Victor said, shaking his head as he watched the crowd. He sat in the rocker with Chris asleep in his arms. "Hasn't *anyone* asked how you pulled off so many elaborate tricks?"

Henry shook his head. "I guess everyone just figured we wouldn't tell anyway."

"Amazing," Victor said.

"Yep." Henry tensed when a woman by the fireplace suddenly looked behind her, as though someone had bumped into her. Of course, no one was there. "Don't you want to put Chris to bed?"

"No." Victor tightened his hold on the toddler. "I'm keeping both boys right where I can see them until your otherworldly visitors are gone."

"Speaking of gone, where did your daughters disappear to?" Henry hadn't seen Paige since he had helped the kids play pin-the-face-on-the-pumpkin over an hour ago.

Victor frowned. "I don't know."

"They're in the kitchen," Coop said. He walked over, stuffing snack plates and crumpled napkins into a trash bag.

"Is something wrong?" Victor asked, shifting uneasily.

"Didn't seem to be," Coop said. "It looked like they were just sitting and talking to a new friend. It's been a long, hard day, and they probably just needed a break."

"A new friend?" Henry couldn't help being suspicious. He was a cop. "Or a new Innocent?"

"She didn't seem upset or frightened." Coop paused thoughtfully. "Neither did Piper, Paige, or Phoebe."

As Henry relaxed, he felt a tug on his tunic. He glanced down at Wyatt and smiled. His young nephew didn't look like the most powerful magical being in existence. "What's up?"

"Can we have the bobbing apples now?" Wyatt asked. Then he frowned slightly and shook his finger. "But no more dunking."

Henry laughed. "No more dunking."

A creeping dread nagged Phoebe as she watched the footprints form. "What is that?"

"*Who* is that," Paige corrected.

"I'm pretty sure it's the ghost that tried to squeeze off Leo's arms." Fiona reached into the pocket of her cape as she slowly stood up. "A bully ghost, to be precise."

"How dangerous is it?" Piper put her feet on the rungs of her chair as the footprints advanced.

"Very," Leo said. "Take my word for it."

"But it's not typical." Fiona stepped away from her chair and paused. "Bully ghosts usually pick on weaker ghosts. This one is trying to terrify us."

"And doing a darn good job," Paige muttered. She removed her Maid Marian head cloth and shook out her hair.

Fiona was easy to read. Phoebe suspected that their mutual psychic abilities made her more sensitive to the other woman's emotional state. Fiona was concerned, but not terrified.

"This guy is a lot more powerful than anything I've run into before." Fiona didn't take her eyes off the footprints. "But what bothers me is, where did it come from and why?"

"Didn't it come through the spell portal?" Piper asked.

"It couldn't have," Paige said. "Ghosts are spirits that haven't moved on to the otherworld yet. They're stuck here because they have unresolved issues."

"Then, shouldn't this one be stuck in the

place it's haunting?" Piper twisted to follow the footprints' progress.

"It should," Fiona said, "but this is All Hallows' Eve. A motivated ghost can go wherever it wants on Halloween."

Phoebe shifted uncomfortably, wondering if the invisible intruder was anyone they knew. They had never killed a human, but there were Innocents they hadn't been able to save. Some criminals had died because of their actions—or inactions.

Fiona moved suddenly, throwing a handful of white crystals on the leading set of watery prints. "Sea salt that's been blessed under a full moon," she explained. "It might diminish the ghost's energies."

"That's one we haven't tried," Paige mused.

"How will we know if it works?" Leo glanced over his shoulder, alerted to someone walking toward the kitchen. As he stood up to intercept, several knives lifted off the counter and zoomed across the room.

"Leo!" Paige instantly orbed the man out of the knives' path, a safer move than trying to redirect multiple blades.

When the knives hit the wall, the tips imbedded in the wood.

A woman walking toward the kitchen bumped into Leo. "Excuse me, Leo. I didn't see you standing there. Have you seen my husband?"

"He's not in here," Leo said, blocking her view of the kitchen. He didn't move until she left.

"Guess the sea salt didn't work." Fiona crossed her arms, looking thoughtful and cha-grined.

"Why did it attack you, Leo?" Piper asked.

Leo shrugged and shook his head. "I don't know."

"Maybe it just wanted to get our attention," Fiona said.

"*That* worked," Piper agreed.

"Or it wanted to stop Leo from leaving," Paige added.

The hair on the back of Phoebe's neck tingled when she sensed the malevolent presence filling the room. It was seething with anger, and they had a house full of Innocents, many of them children.

"Or he was a random target," Fiona said.

Phoebe jumped out of her seat. "We have to get the ghost out of here."

"We can't vanquish it without—"

Phoebe cut Piper off. "I know, but maybe we can use a spell to evict it. If it's not inside, the guests will be safe. Especially the children."

"Okay." Paige nodded. "Which one of you has an evict-a-ghost spell?"

Piper focused on Phoebe. "The spell-o-matic is on the blink, so I hope you can think fast."

Vanquishing ghosts was an extremely difficult and dangerous magical task. Phoebe had no illusions that evicting one would be easy or even possible, but they had to try. She took a small pad and pen from a drawer and closed her eyes. When she had a rhyme, she scribbled it down and motioned her sisters over. She hoped chanting the hastily composed spell with the Power of Three would enhance it enough to work.

> *Watery-footprint ghost, be gone,*
> *With the Power of Three we roust*
> *You out the door and onto the lawn,*
> *Get out and stay out of this house.*

When they finished, Phoebe held her breath.

"If this doesn't work, we'll have to evacuate the Manor," Piper said.

Phoebe ducked, her reflexes kicking in a split second before she was skewered by a metal apple corer. The spell had failed.

"What went wrong?" Paige asked.

"Ghosts are exceptionally powerful on Halloween," Fiona said. "And this one is probably highly motivated."

"Piper!" Leo yelled. "Look out!"

Piper leaned forward, but not far or fast enough. The apple corer yanked a curl out of her dark wig as it zinged past. "Hey! That's rented hair!"

Every utensil on the prep island flew across the room, flung by the unknown ghost.

"Get down, Fiona!" Phoebe dropped to the floor. The ghost hunter crumpled into a brown velour heap beside her and covered her head with her arms.

The air vibrated as knives and spoons sliced through it at blinding speeds. No one was hurt in the first barrage, but the missiles adjusted their trajectories as they circled for a second attack.

Piper froze the airborne items, but the ghost launched another volley.

"Piper!" Leo ordered, his voice tight. "Stay down."

Piper stretched out on the floor, but the hoop under her colonial dress stood up, raising the skirt like a sail. A paring knife tore through the fabric. "Now I definitely won't get my deposit back."

"Forget the money," Leo said. "Crawl!"

Muttering under her breath, Piper started to inch toward Leo. Phoebe shared her anger and frustration. Her not being able to freeze the ghost gave it an edge.

A blade flew past Phoebe's ear, so close she could hear the metal sing. A spoon nicked her arm as it arrowed into the floor. From her low vantage point, she saw Paige's crimson skirt swirl into sparkling light.

When Paige appeared beside Leo, the ghost hurled pots, pans, and other cookware toward the doorway. Leo held up a hand to deflect a plastic measuring cup. It hit his palm with such force, he winced.

Paige dodged a metal pie plate, then held out her hand to mount a rescue.

"Fiona first!" Phoebe looked up so the words wouldn't be muffled.

Fiona was still lying facedown with her arms clamped over her head. The ghost hunter's breathing was slow and steady. *Scared, but not panicked*, Phoebe thought as Paige orbed the woman into the space behind Leo. Saucepans, lids, cups, and spoons struck the ceiling and the walls.

Fiona glanced up, disoriented and confused by her sudden displacement. "Did I just turn into a million sparkles?"

"It feels weird at first," Leo said, "but you get used to it."

Piper's stand-up hoop skirt was like a blue and gold flag, taunting the enraged ghost as she continued to crawl across the floor. All the flying objects in the kitchen suddenly swerved toward the brocade target.

"Piper!" Paige lost no time saving her sister.

Phoebe held her breath as Fiona scooted backward on hands and knees, trying to get out of the way. Reacting instinctively, she didn't realize that Paige could pinpoint Piper's landing. Paige compensated and dropped Piper into the empty spot between Fiona and Leo.

"Are you okay?" Leo squatted down and

helped Piper into a sitting position. Her wig
was askew, and a sole ringlet hung down over
one eye.

"I'm as okay as possible for someone whose
kitchen is being wrecked by a berserk ghost."
Piper tore off the wig and scratched behind
her ear.

Phoebe stayed flattened and motionless,
waiting her turn and hoping that no one beyond
the short hallway had seen the light show.
Bizarre noises, cold winds, and flickering lights
could be explained. They could probably even
come up with a logical reason why they were all
huddled in the cramped space by the kitchen
door. But there was no acceptable explanation
for people that vanished and reappeared in
bursts of glorious light.

A cookie cutter hit Phoebe's back just before
Paige orbed her out of the kitchen. The tiny teeth
bit through the western shirt and sank into her
skin. As her body dissolved into orb particles, all
she could think about was going through life
with a pumpkin-shaped scar.

"Ow!" Phoebe winced with pain when she
materialized.

Behind her, pots, pans, and metal utensils
clattered, rolled, and clanged as they suddenly
dropped to the floor. A crystal serving bowl
shattered. Suddenly, the room grew cold and
quiet.

"Is it gone?" Leo asked.

"I wouldn't count on that," Piper said.

"Phoebe's bleeding." Fiona inhaled sharply when she saw the metal pumpkin clinging to Phoebe's back. "Where's the first-aid kit?"

"Right here," Paige turned and knelt down. "This is going to sting."

"Just fix it." Phoebe gritted her teeth as Paige carefully removed the cookie cutter. The wonder emanating from Fiona was as soothing to her nerves as Paige's healing power was on her flesh. "No scar, right?"

"No scar," Paige assured her.

"Do you have a card, Paige?" Fiona asked.

"No," Paige admitted, "but I'll give you my cell phone number."

Phoebe smiled. A psychic ghost hunter might someday need the Whitelighter's ability to heal injuries caused by supernatural evil.

Someone in the sunroom screamed. More shrieks followed the sound of breaking glass and a loud crash.

"The kids!" Phoebe scrambled to her feet. Wyatt could protect himself and Chris with his shield, but Abbey, Vanessa, and Ryan were defenseless.

"We have to clear the house—now," Piper said. She motioned for Leo to follow her through the dining room and into the hall.

"How are you doing, Fiona?" Paige asked. "This is probably more than you bargained for, so if you want to bail—"

"And miss out on the ghost hunt of a life-time?" Fiona exclaimed. "Not a chance."

As Phoebe started toward the sunroom, the dining room floor undulated under her feet. Losing her balance, she stumbled against the wall and braced herself until the wooden waves subsided.

A couple dressed as comic-book superheroes stood by the buffet table. Their plates flipped into the air as their feet flew out from under them. Canapés, cookies, and raw vegetables rained down as they fell.

"C'mon, folks." Struggling to stay upright, Paige held on to the table and grabbed the woman's hand to help her up. "Major rupture in the plumbing. Party's over."

A cucumber sandwich peeled off the man's costume as he wobbled to his feet. He scooped a glob of cheese spread off his sleeve and flicked it at the floor.

"Bye, now." Paige shoved the couple into the hall. The foyer floor was flat, and they raced for the front door.

Phoebe saw Abbey pull Vanessa aside in the sunroom. One of the planters toppled onto the spot where the younger girl had been standing. Both girls darted behind a wicker chair, under which O'Brien and Ryan were already huddled.

Victor stood over Wyatt and Chris, trying to obstruct the guests' view. His attempt to hide the evidence of magic was unnecessary. Everyone was too entertained or freaked out by the chaos to notice the faint glow of the shield protecting them.

As the floor settled, Phoebe, Paige, and Fiona dashed into the sunroom. A low moaning sound became a pitiful wail.

"Wow! That is so cool!" A teenager jerked back as a plasma ball passed inches in front of his face. The fiery sphere hit the drapes, setting them on fire.

In the confusion, no one noticed anything unusual when the flaming drapes orbed off the rods into a pile on the floor. Paige waved frantically at Coop and pointed. He pulled half-empty glasses from a side table and turned them over to douse the fire.

"Was that lightning?" Fiona asked, amazed.

"Plasma ball," Phoebe whispered. "From the ghostly plane. Ghosts use it as a weapon."

"Plasma, ghostly plane, weapon," Fiona said, committing the words to memory. "Remind me to ask you more about that when this is over."

"Sure," Phoebe said, nodding as she tried to break through a knot of guests to reach O'Brien and the children. "That's the way out." She pointed toward the living room.

"Great party." A neighbor handed Phoebe his empty plate and glass. "You'll be hard-pressed to top it next year."

"But we sure hope you try," his wife added.

She took his arm just as a grating groan built to another chilling crescendo.

As the couple left, Phoebe scanned the room.

Paige orbed another plasma ball into the fireplace before it hit a caveman holding a child in a bunny suit.

"Fireworks!" The little rabbit clapped her hands, thrilled. The father was petrified with fear.

Fiona rushed over and hurried them across the room, waving others toward the door as they passed. "Sorry, folks. Show's over!"

Paige stepped back to avoid being trampled by a very large man bolting for the hall. A loud group in the corner seemed oblivious to the sudden exodus. They kept talking, laughing, and sipping their drinks.

Encased in Wyatt's expanded shield, Victor carried Chris and held Wyatt's hand as he trundled them into the living room. The surface of the protective barrier rippled and bubbled, as though something was trying to break through it. The effect stopped when grandfather and grandchildren reached the hall and turned toward the front door.

Setting the dirty dishes down, Phoebe studied the fleeing guests. Ghostly winds whipped hair and clothes until each person crossed an invisible threshold near the front door. That was probably important, but she couldn't focus on it now. The children's safety came first.

Hiding her anxiety behind a bright smile,

Phoebe ducked down by O'Brien. "Hey, kids! How you doing?"

"I'm scared." Vanessa pressed against Abbey.

"You're supposed to be scared on Halloween, Vanessa." Abbey's voice was calm despite the uncertainty in her eyes. "The lightning balls are just a trick. Right, Phoebe?"

"Yeah!" Phoebe agreed. "Pretty good, huh?"

"This is the best haunted house I've ever been in," Ryan said. "Are you going to do this again next year?"

"I certainly hope not." O'Brien glared at Phoebe. "What in blazes is going on?"

"It's the grand finale." Phoebe shot the leprechaun a pleading look, silently begging him to play along. Their lives were in danger, but she didn't want to traumatize the kids if she didn't have to.

A new plasma ball appeared out of thin air and sped toward Coop and Henry. Paige spun to deflect it, but her timing lagged. The fiery ball skimmed Henry's head.

"That was a little too close," Henry said, whistling as he ran his hand over his singed hair.

"Radical!" A young man standing beside the two men grinned. He was dressed as a biker in leather jacket and jeans with slicked-back hair. "I don't know who does your pyrotechnics, but they're awesome."

"Time to go." Paige motioned for the man to move out.

"It's early yet." He looked at his watch, unaware of several plasma balls that flared into view and hurtled toward him.

There were too many to deflect, leaving Paige no choice. She orbed the man two feet to the side, out of the line of fire.

When the man finished materializing, he looked up with a puzzled expression. "Did I miss something?"

"The door's that way." Henry pointed the man toward the hall and gave him a push to get him moving. "Thanks for coming!"

Although paralyzed with shock for a moment, Abbey recovered with an excited "Wow! How did she do that?"

"It's magic," O'Brien said.

"Really?" Ryan's eyes widened.

"It's a really great *trick*," Abbey insisted, impressed but still skeptical.

"Can she do it again?" Vanessa asked.

Phoebe noticed black splotches moving toward them across the ceiling. A whispering echo grew louder and the flooring underneath the ghostly blight turned to dust. She had to act quickly before the next "special effect" hurt someone. "Close your eyes, and I'll show you another one you won't believe."

All three children squeezed their eyes closed.

Phoebe whispered to O'Brien, "Get these kids outside. My father will watch them until I get there."

"Aye, and I will." O'Brien wrapped his short arms around the children.

"Paige!" Phoebe yelled. "Four to go!"

As Paige whirled, a plasma ball grazed her shoulder. She staggered back a step.

Phoebe glanced upward. The children had mere seconds to escape the dehydrating effects of the ghost's advance. "Get ready to run!" Her words hung in the air as Paige orbed the leprechaun and his charges to safety in the hall.

Phoebe jumped back. The sawdust trail stopped abruptly, and the black marks faded from the ceiling.

"Hey!" Abbey exclaimed when she opened her eyes and found herself in the hall. "That was unbelievable."

"That was magic," Vanessa said gravely.

O'Brien hustled the children to the door and pointed outside. Toward Victor, Phoebe assumed. She exhaled with relief when the kids raced out, then frowned when Abbey turned back to hug the leprechaun. The girl's arms couldn't pass through a transparent barrier that blocked the opening.

Did the ghost want to keep someone out or in? Phoebe tucked the disturbing question away until later, and turned her attention back to the evacuation.

Except for the oblivious talkers, the sunroom was guest-free. The stragglers resisted Coop's polite attempts to make them vacate, but they changed their minds when Henry ordered them out in his cop voice. Phoebe didn't hear the woman whimper until the noisy group was gone.

She found Fran lying on the floor in the corner.

The terrified woman curled up and covered her eyes when Phoebe touched her shoulder. "Go away! I don't care if you haunt silver teapots forever! Just leave me alone!"

"It's Phoebe, Fran. You have to get out of here."

"I can't." Fran whispered, peeking through her fingers. "She's waiting to get me."

There *was* a ghost waiting. Just not the one Fran imagined. Despite the dangers, the circumstances presented Phoebe with an opportunity that might not come again.

"Maybe if you promise to stop trying to contact Edward in the afterlife," Phoebe said, "she'll leave."

"Will that work?" Fran lowered her hands. Her eyes were red from crying.

"I am absolutely positive that if you go home and forget about ghosts, they'll forget about you." With a wary eye out for the real ghost, Phoebe urged the woman to her feet. Fran *would* be fine, as soon as she got out of the Manor.

"But what about Edward?" Fran asked as Phoebe walked her through the house to the hall.

"You've got to start living the rest of your

life," Phoebe said, gently pushing Fran out the front door. "That's what Edward would want."

Paige stood with Fiona and O'Brien by the settee in the hall. One shoulder of her red costume was charred, but she didn't appeared to be badly injured. Overhearing Phoebe's comment to Fran, she clasped her hands and mouthed a thank-you.

Fran scurried down the stone steps as if she couldn't get away from the house fast enough. Phoebe doubted she'd return to harass them about ghosts anytime soon, if ever.

Many of the other guests had stopped in the yard to admire the outdoor decorations. Henry stood with the talky people, soaking up their praise for the Halloween display. Victor kept his gaze on the kids while he carried on a conversation with a neighbor. Vanessa, Ryan, and Wyatt chased one another around the tombstones, squealing. Abbey sat with Chris in front of a talking skeleton, listening to it repeat a string of spooky phrases.

"Thanks for coming!" Piper smiled and waved from the door, then lowered her voice. "Would you believe this party was a huge hit?"

"As near as I can tell, everyone thinks we put on a fantastic show." Leo took off his commodore coat and hung it on the coat rack with his hat. "I'll go check the kids."

"Wait—" Before Phoebe could stop him, Leo stepped through the doorway.

"Is there a problem?" Piper asked.

I'm not sure," Phoebe said. "Try coming back inside, Leo." As she expected, an invisible barrier kept him out.

"Did the ghost do that?" Paige asked.

Coop followed up. "If it did, does it want to keep Leo out, or does it want all of us gone?"

"It wouldn't let Abbey back in either," Phoebe said.

Leo glanced over his shoulder. "So Henry, Victor, and the boys are stuck outside too."

"I assume so, but I don't know." Phoebe frowned. Fiona, O'Brien, Coop, and her sisters were the only people left inside the Manor with her. "And that's a problem. If the ghost wants us out, it wants us out for a reason."

Paige folded her arms. "I'm not going anywhere until I get some answers. Maybe not even then."

"No ghost is kicking me out of my house," Piper said.

Phoebe noticed that Fiona was frowning. "What?"

"This ghost is stronger than I thought possible," Fiona said. "It's frightening. But I'm not going anywhere either," she quickly added.

"I'm stayin' with the pretty Irish miss." O'Brien gazed at Fiona with adoring eyes.

Fiona pretended not to notice.

Paige's flower arrangement suddenly flew down the hall and smashed against the doorjamb near Piper's head. Eyes flashing, Piper whirled to challenge the invisible culprit. "That won't get rid of me, bozo! It'll just make me madder."

"Is this ghost stronger than Olivia, Paige?" Phoebe asked. Killed by her fiancé's brother and bent on his family's destruction, Olivia Calloway had reignited an old family feud with the Montanas.

"It sure feels like it," Paige said, "and that's not good. Olivia was obsessed with revenge. That's how she got so powerful. We don't know what's driving this one, but it must be something big."

"How many ghosts have you known?" Fiona asked.

"With the new guy"—Phoebe scowled—"one too many."

"Speakin' of the ghost, shouldn't we be decidin' what to do about it?" O'Brien asked.

"First things first." Piper stepped up to where Leo stood. "Take Victor and the kids back to his apartment."

"And take Henry with you," Paige said.

"And use a cell phone to call Abbey's parents," Phoebe added. "You can drop her and the Moreno kids off on your way."

Leo nodded, but he didn't want to leave them. He lowered his voice so only Piper could hear. "You might need help from someone on the outside."

"Then I'll call," Piper whispered. "We've handled ghosts before. I'm sure we can take care of this one."

Piper ducked as another shriek reverberated through the hall. A plasma ball barely missed her and hit the barrier. It disintegrated on impact, and the high-pitched wail receded.

"We'll be fine," Piper said. She stayed in the doorway until Victor drove away from the curb. Then she looked at everyone in turn. "Anyone else want to call it quits?"

No one did, but Phoebe felt momentarily overwhelmed. Fear laced Fiona's excitement. Infatuation riddled the leprechaun's apprehension. Piper and Paige worried about Leo, Henry, and the boys. Coop was worried about her.

Piper closed the front door, and Phoebe took a few seconds to purge the stronger feelings so she could think clearly. The intrusion of a cold, calculating, and unfamiliar mindset caught her completely off guard.

Assistant Professor Ken Carson walked out of the living room, clapping his hands slowly. "I have to hand it to you people. I've seen some elaborate hoax hauntings, but this was the best."

Chapter Seven

"Ken Carson, I presume?" Piper hadn't had a personal run-in with Fiona's academic nemesis at the party, but everything about the man confirmed her sisters' opinions: He was a smug, know-it-all jerk.

Ken cast a condescending glance at the ghost hunter. "Apparently, Fiona has already brought our opposing positions on the matter of ghosts to your attention."

"She has," Piper said. "*And* she has the facts on her side."

"Facts?" Ken threw back his head with a derisive laugh. "You want me to believe a ghost was responsible for tonight's madness?"

"That would be wise," Paige said. "It's true."

Phoebe nodded. "And this particular ghost has a serious grudge against *some*body about *some*thing."

"You should leave." Piper opened the front door again.

"Yes," Fiona agreed, "you should."

"You've taken me along on other hunts, Fiona. Is there something about this *haunting*"—Ken put a sarcastic emphasis on the word—"you don't want me to see?"

"I let you tag along before because I wanted to prove to you that ghosts are real," Fiona said. "But you can't—or won't—see the evidence that's right in front of you."

Ken rolled his eyes. "Like spinning compass dials, strange noises, and mysterious holes that appear out of nowhere? All of this evidence has logical explanations."

"Mind your tone, lad," O'Brien warned.

Piper followed the exchange with interest. The Charmed Ones kept their powers secret to protect their normal lives. Fiona dealt with public ridicule from people like Ken Carson because they *didn't* believe. *And apparently,* Piper thought, *skeptics won't accept anything that might prove them wrong.*

"Sometimes a ghost is the only explanation that makes sense." Fiona spoke as though resigned to the futility of trying to convince him.

"So what's the problem here?" Ken glanced at the sisters. "Afraid I'll figure out how you managed your magnificent parlor tricks?"

"No," Coop said, "we're afraid you'll get hurt."

"Don't waste your breath trying to scare me off," Ken shot back. "It won't work.

Phoebe fixed the professor with a hard stare. "You are a very foolish man."

"And you're dressed as a rodeo rider," Ken snidely pointed out. "Why should I take you seriously?"

"Because there really *is* a threat, Ken," Fiona said. "Spirits *like* to mess with skeptics. They'll do whatever they can to prove their existence. And this one isn't playing."

"You do *not* want to tangle with this ghost," Piper said.

"I suppose you're *dead* certain of that." Ken smirked, enjoying his joke.

Fiona threw up her hands.

"Honestly, yes," Paige snapped.

Ken shrugged. "I'm not leaving until Fiona does."

"Fine!" Annoyed, Piper turned to close the door. In the glow of the streetlight, she saw a boy start to run up the stone steps. The late trick-or-treater was dressed in camouflage sweats and a torn white T-shirt streaked with fake blood.

At least I hope it's fake, Piper fretted as the boy's father dashed up the steps after him. The child stopped suddenly, then made a sharp left. The man chased him across the yard through the decorative tombstones, back to the sidewalk, and down the street. With soldier costumes being so popular this year, she hoped she wouldn't have trouble finding new camouflage sweatpants for Wyatt.

"You'll regret that decision, Ken," Fiona said. "I wouldn't even try to confront this ghost on my own."

"Then there's nothing to worry about," Ken said. "You've got three girls, a cowboy, and a dwarf for backup."

"Who are you calling a dwarf?" O'Brien huffed.

Paige nudged him to shut up.

Piper didn't have a no-worries option. They had two Innocents and a leprechaun to protect, and her powers against the unknown spirit were limited. As though to underscore the disconcerting situation, the door blew open again the instant she closed it.

"Nice." Ken's cocky smile changed to perplexed surprise when an unseen force pushed him toward the open door. "What the—"

Piper quickly assessed the Ken complication. It certainly seemed as though the ghost wanted them out of the house, which meant they had to stay to figure out why. And although she'd rather not, they had to include Ken. The professor couldn't be trusted to go home and forget about everything. He would want to flaunt his findings. An academic article debunking a Halliwell ghost could be just as disruptive as one that claimed the Manor was a haunted house. Besides, they couldn't protect Ken from the malicious spirit if he stayed to spy on them from the outside.

Piper slammed the door closed again.

The shoving stopped, and Ken sputtered, "Who pushed me?" When Fiona tried to answer, he cut her short. "Do not say it."

"Listen." Paige walked up to Ken and jabbed him in the chest with her finger. "I don't care if you believe there's a ghost or not. In fact, I'll be just as glad if you leave here thinking that everything you're about to see is some kind of trick. But take a hint. Do what we tell you, and maybe you won't get killed. Got it?" She didn't wait for an answer. "Good."

"Ditto that." Phoebe jabbed Ken's chest when Paige moved away.

"And show a wee bit more respect for the ladies." O'Brien glared at the professor, hands planted on his hips.

A shadow of dismay crossed Ken's face. It wasn't because he believed a ghost had pushed him, Piper realized. Paige's outburst had given him pause. He probably thought they were all crazy, which was preferable to knowing they were witches. His misconceptions wouldn't last if he witnessed their efforts to vanquish the ghost, and there was little chance of preventing that. Of course, considering Fiona's remarks and his responses so far, he might not believe *anything* he saw.

"So where do we start?" Paige asked.

Piper didn't hesitate. "I'm going to change into more comfortable clothes. Then we'll vanq . . . get rid of the . . . oh, whatever."

"I'm with you on the clothes." Paige looked down at her Maid Marian gown. "I am *so* glad Henry and I changed into our costumes upstairs."

"Coop and I drove over in costume, and I didn't bring any regular clothes to change into." Sighing, Phoebe held out the sides of her western skirt. "This isn't the best ghost hunting outfit, but at least we decided not to come as Tarzan and Jane."

"Are we sure this ghost is evil?" Coop asked.

"Cookie cutter in the back?" Phoebe turned to show off the tiny punctures in her shirt. "It's a bad guy."

"Could I take a closer look at that?" Ken asked.

"Knock yourself out." Phoebe turned to let Ken examine the fabric. He wasn't looking when the ghost hurled several shards of broken glass down the long hall. Paige orbed the sharp projectiles aside. They shattered when they struck the woodwork.

Ken looked up as a plasma ball fizzled out in midair. He blinked and shook his head. "You'd better have that electrical outlet checked."

"Which electrical outlet is that?" Paige asked. "The one hanging—"

Piper motioned her sister to be quiet. As much as she wanted to help Fiona establish credibility with her critic, the Manor couldn't be involved.

"That was lame." Phoebe glanced at Fiona.

"The ghost's energies are probably drained," Fiona said, "but it just needs time to recharge."

"How long?" Phoebe asked.

"I have no idea," Fiona admitted.

"Then we can't waste any time." Piper turned to Phoebe. "You and Coop take everyone . . . somewhere while Paige and I go upstairs to change. We'll get the Book."

"We'll be in the kitchen," Phoebe said as she and Coop ushered everyone out.

"You wouldn't happen to have more cider?" O'Brien asked Phoebe. "My throat's a mite parched."

"I could go for some of that." Ken patted O'Brien's head as he sauntered by.

That was probably worth a year of bad luck. Piper smiled as Paige orbed them into the attic.

Paige didn't usually wear T-shirts and sweat-pants outside her own home unless she was jog-ging. It was just a stroke of luck that she had worn something comfortable and functional tonight. Henry didn't want anyone outside the party to see him dressed up as Robin Hood, so he had insisted on changing into costume at the Manor.

The small spirits hovering above the grains of rice on the hall floor scattered as Paige walked through, and they closed ranks when she ducked into the bathroom. She applied ointment to the minor plasma burn on her shoulder, then walked back across the hall to get Piper and the Book of Shadows.

Piper had changed into a tank top, cotton drawstring pants, and sneakers. She handed Paige the Book and picked up a spare set of casual clothes and shoes. "For Phoebe."

"Good idea," Paige said. "One less thing for Ken to insult is one less temptation to do something I'll regret later."

Piper smiled. "I'm almost sorry Coop's not as likely as Leo and Henry to throw a punch."

"We also have to stop worrying about what we say around Ken." Paige moved closer to orb them both back downstairs. "I don't want to guess what you're trying to tell me. A mistake could be fatal."

Piper sighed heavily. "I know, you're right. I just hate the thought of letting that pompous weasel know our secrets."

"Maybe instead of trying to hide what we're doing we should play it up," Paige suggested. "The more over the top, the better. He already thinks we're charlatans—or fools."

"He *wants* to think we're fools." Piper smiled as the brilliance of the tactic sank in. "His arrogant, narrow-minded pea-brain will latch onto anything that proves his theory and dismiss everything that doesn't."

"It could work." Paige smiled. "The professor saw a sparking electrical outlet suspended three feet off the ground in the hall because he had to make sense of something that seemed impossible."

"*Assistant* professor," Piper said with a sly grin as Paige orbed them out.

Piper gasped the instant she materialized in the living room. "Look at this mess!"

"It's been worse," Paige said. Torn streamers, burned drapes, discarded paper cups and plates, dust, and scorch marks could easily be cleaned up and fixed. After the Hollow battle between the Charmed Ones and the Jenkins sisters, a temporal do-over had been required to reverse the Manor's destruction.

"Yeah," Piper agreed. "At least the house is still standing."

"There's no point cleaning up until our mystery ghost is banished or vanquished," Paige said as she walked toward the kitchen.

The dining room was less cluttered. Everything had been cleared off the buffet table except two platters of snacks and the centerpiece. The remaining refreshments were on the center island in the kitchen. Fiona was packing leftovers in plastic storage containers. The floor was still littered with pots, pans, and utensils.

"Thanks for cleaning up," Piper said.

"You're welcome," Fiona said.

"I thought it might be safer to get all the silverware and other potentially lethal objects into one room." Phoebe dumped a dustpan full of broken glass into a trash bag.

As long as we don't stay in the kitchen where the ghost can use them against us, Paige thought.

Piper groaned as she scanned the debris.

Phoebe tried to console her. "I don't think you lost that much."

Coop picked up a stack of lids and pie tins and set them in the sink. He had taken off his hat and neck scarf and looked more like a country Californian than a movie cowboy caricature.

Ken sat at the head of the table, eating cookies.

O'Brien shuffled through the litter, searching for survivors. He held up a large aluminum spoon. The rounded end was dented. "Will you be wantin' to keep this?"

Piper took the spoon and turned it over in her hand. "This is my favorite. I use it for everything."

"Which makes me wonder why you battered something with it just to make your friends believe that your house is haunted." Ken chewed, waiting for an answer.

"I didn't," Piper said. "The ghost did."

A stack of metal mixing bowls fell off the island.

"I suppose you want me to believe the ghost did that, too." Ken looked at Fiona.

"I really don't care what you believe, Ken." Fiona retrieved the bowls. "It just doesn't matter. Not anymore."

"But other things matter a lot," Paige said. "The ghost is getting its strength back, and we still have to figure out the best way to defeat it."

"There's more than one way?" Ken asked.

Piper gave Phoebe the everyday clothes and whispered in her ear, cluing her in on the plan to stymie Ken by playing on his stubborn assumptions.

"Let's discuss this in the dining room, where there's less chance of being shish-kebobbed." Paige couldn't think straight while she was worried about being stabbed by a kitchen knife and burned to a crisp with plasma.

"Be there in a sec." Phoebe ducked into the pantry to change. Coop waited for her by the pantry door.

Piper sighed as she dropped the dented spoon in the trash and walked out with Paige, Fiona, and O'Brien. Ken hung back to get another plate of food.

Paige set the Book of Shadows down at the head of the table. They had moved the chairs against the walls so guests could walk around the buffet. As Paige reached to pull one back, a force yanked it out of her grasp. Instead of flinging the chair, the ghost dropped it.

"It must be conserving its strength," Fiona said as the others walked in from the kitchen.

O'Brien tugged a chair over for Fiona, then climbed onto a second beside her. The ghost hunter hid an amused smile.

"What did we miss?" Ken sat down with his snacks. "Did Casper blow another fuse?"

Everyone ignored him.

"We don't know how long it will take the ghost to recharge," Fiona said. "What if it's only minutes? Don't you have something to keep it at bay until we settle on a plan?" She shifted her gaze from one witch to the next. "A charm or a talisman?"

"I wish," Paige said. She flipped open the Book to the page she had compiled on ghosts.

"Some Chinese people use a little dragon thingie that protects homes from ghosts," Piper said. "It kept Mark out of his mom's house."

"Mark?" Fiona arched an eyebrow.

"The ghost Piper dated for a day so the Chinese gatekeeper couldn't steal his soul before he was properly buried," Phoebe explained.

"Why not use the dragon thingie?" O'Brien asked.

"We don't have one." Piper moved the discussion on.

"Which leaves us with three options." Paige ran her finger down the page in the Book of Shadows, refreshing her memory.

"Do you mind if I take notes?" Ken pulled a compact electronic device out of his pocket.

"Oh, for the love of—" Piper froze the room. She took the device out of Ken's hand, removed the battery, and put the device back. When the scene sped up, she smiled. "No, go right ahead."

Ken punched a button on the device's keypad and frowned when nothing happened.

For Fiona's benefit, Paige reviewed the known ways to vanquish or neutralize a ghost. "We can pour a mandrake root potion on the grave, remove the object of its obsession, or cast the vanquishing spell from the ghostly plane."

"But every option has a downside," Phoebe cautioned.

"Can't wait to hear." Ken slipped his gadget back into his pocket and picked up another sandwich.

"Then be quiet and listen," Coop said evenly. The only hint of irritation was a slight flexing of his square jaw.

Paige continued. "We don't know where the ghost's body is buried or what's keeping it earthbound."

"And you have to be dead to cast a spell from the ghostly plane," Piper added. "But, believe it or not, that's our best bet."

Ken sat up. "Who's going to volunteer to die?"

"Not me," Piper said. "Been there, done that. If I were a cat, I'd only have four or five lives left."

Paige couldn't resist needling Ken a little more. "We'll summon Grams. She's been dead for years."

"I'm *dying* to meet her," Ken said without missing a beat.

Fiona shifted in her seat. She didn't say anything, but Paige could tell that the prospect of calling another spirit disturbed her. However, the barrier between the living and the dead was already open. The damage was done, and they needed a dead person to say the spell.

"Ready?" Paige asked her sisters.

Nodding, Piper and Phoebe recited the familiar incantation along with her.

> *Hear these words, hear our cry,*
> *Spirit from the other side,*
> *Come to us, we summon thee,*
> *Cross now the great divide.*

Paige braced herself to mollify the elder Halliwell witch when she arrived. As much as Grams loved her granddaughters, she might not be thrilled to see them on Halloween, in the company of a leprechaun, a ghost hunter, and a disagreeable skeptic.

Ken looked around expectantly, then tensed. "Did you hear that? Someone said, 'Get out or die.'"

Although Paige wouldn't put it past the ghost to whisper in Ken's ear, no one else had heard anything.

After several seconds when no one appeared, Ken checked his watch. "Looks like Grams is a no-show."

"The spell must have failed," Phoebe said. "Otherwise she'd be here."

"But I used it just a few hours ago to call O'Brien's friends," Paige said.

"Maybe that's the problem." Piper drummed her fingers on the table. "Most spirits have been trapped in the otherworld for hundreds of years. Paige probably started a spiritual stampede when she lowered the barrier."

Paige squinted, thinking out loud. "So the flow of spiritual entities might be so thick and intense, a spell can't get through."

"Is that possible, Coop?" Phoebe asked.

Ken looked at Coop askance. "Is he some kind of expert?"

"He's a Cupid," O'Brien said. "Better watch it, or he'll make you fall in love with a cranky old crone."

"Don't tempt me, O'Brien." Exhaling, Coop lapsed into a moment of deep thought. When he looked up, his expression was grim. "The spell must have been blocked. Grams wouldn't ignore a summons."

"Then Liam or Seamus or Marty will have to cast the spell," O'Brien said. "As soon as they get back."

Plasma balls exploded from the fireplace, showering the table with sparks. Ken frantically brushed burning flakes off his sweater as the spheres hit the wall. Halloween knickknacks and dishes of candy bounced off the sideboard. The floor vibrated under their feet, and a screeching whine reverberated off the walls.

"Earthquake!" Ken yelled and ran for the hall doorway. His spontaneous reaction to the tremor was ingrained in every longtime resident of San Francisco.

Although the ghost was probably responsible, Coop, Phoebe, and Piper sought refuge in the kitchen doorway. Pieces of plaster broke off the ceiling, and O'Brien pulled Fiona to safety under the table. He smiled as they hunkered down side by side.

Prompted by her concern for an Innocent, Paige huddled with Ken. The leprechauns would be out celebrating Samhain until just before dawn, but she wasn't sure they could hold out that long. Despite the need to regenerate its energies, the ghost seemed to be getting stronger.

Chapter Eight

Phoebe leaned against Coop and covered her ears to muffle the bone-rattling roar of the enraged ghost. Books flew off shelves and lamps crashed to the floor. The massive dining room table thumped as it repeatedly rose and fell back onto the wooden floor. Now locked in a protective embrace, Fiona and O'Brien winced every time the table legs hit.

"Look out!" Coop pulled Phoebe and Piper down and out of the strike zone of another plasma ball.

In the hall doorway, Paige deflected a barrage of molten spheres. She missed one. The plasma ball seared the back of Ken's neck as it sailed into the hall and hit an ancestor's portrait on the wall. The frame burst into flames.

"Save that painting!" Piper yelled.

"Watch it!" Ken snapped. "You scratched me."

"Sorry," Paige said. As she orbed the canvas clear of the burning frame, another plasma ball exploded the glass chimney of an antique hurricane sconce. That was a loss, but she recovered in time to orb the Book of Shadows before it could slide off the table. "Phoebe!" Paige shouted. "Catch!"

The Book appeared in Phoebe's hands just as the floor suddenly curved upward and snapped, like a rug being jerked out from under her. Still clutching the Warren witches' magical tome, Phoebe was pitched into the dining room with her husband and older sister.

Across the room, a violent blast of cold wind blew Paige and Ken out of the doorway and into the hall. Rippling waves in the floor caused Fiona and the leprechaun to begin tumbling toward the door. O'Brien braced himself between the table legs, using his stocky body as a barrier to keep Fiona from rolling out from under it. The ghost roared and slammed into O'Brien, sending the little man sprawling.

"Stop it!" Piper yelled.

Phoebe gasped, staggered by the force of Piper's fury.

"Who are you?" Piper demanded. "What do you want?"

"It's trying to herd us out," Coop said.

"That's not gonna happen." Grabbing a fistful of Ken's sweater, Paige orbed back into the dining room. Shaken and pale, the professor crouched beside her with his eyes closed and his head buried in his arms.

"But why?" Piper dug into the carpet with her fingers. The ghost tried to shake her loose.

"Maybe we should ask." On her knees, Phoebe held the Book of Shadows against her chest. Plaster dust from the broken ceiling billowed around the table.

"A séance?" Piper asked. As she gripped Coop's outstretched hand, all the ghost's efforts stopped abruptly. Everyone was left disoriented and breathless for a moment.

"Is it over?" Ken cautiously raised his head.

"Until the ghost builds up enough energy for an encore." Piper pulled herself into a sitting position and brushed her hair out of her face.

"Also known as an aftershock," Ken countered.

"Whatever," Phoebe said. Although it would be better for them if Ken's skepticism prevailed, his inability to grasp the obvious was exasperating. He was not a stupid man, but his blind faith in his flawed convictions made him act like one.

Paige got the conversation back on track. "If we can figure out the ghost's identity, we might be able to use one of the other two options—"

"Wait!" Phoebe interrupted. "It's probably not a good idea to tell the you-know-what our plans."

Fiona wasn't worried. "That won't matter. The ghost is focused entirely on its own circumstances. It doesn't care about anything that's not directly connected to what it wants."

"But it stopped trying to shake the house apart when we mentioned a séance," Piper said.

"Could be a coincidence." Fiona rubbed a sore spot on her hip.

"Or it *wants* to be contacted." Phoebe eased out from under the table and stood up. "Nothing coincidental ever happens to us."

"I've never been to a séance," Ken said, sending Fiona an accusing glance. "What do we do? Is it just like in the movies?"

Everyone eyed Ken suspiciously.

"Did you run out of insults and caustic remarks?" Paige asked sarcastically.

"No," Ken said, "but if the aftershock is worse than the quake, I want to *die* laughing."

Piper groaned.

"The dead jokes are really getting old," Fiona said, echoing Phoebe's thoughts.

"Let's do this before the ghost attacks again." Phoebe breathed in deeply to collect herself. It had been a while since she had conducted a séance, and she didn't want to forget anything. "Paige, we need five large white candles, a sage stick, and an incense burner from the attic."

"Coming right up." Paige ducked into the hall and out of Ken's sight before she orbed. During the few minutes she was gone, the others cleared broken plaster off the table. The chairs had fallen over during the ghost's rampage. They moved them back into position around the table.

Fiona and Ken both watched attentively as Phoebe arranged the candles in a five-point pattern on the table. She lit the candles, then the sage incense, and nodded for Coop to turn off the lights. Although they could summon family members on their own, the Power of Three was needed to call a strong, perhaps reluctant spirit.

When the Charmed Ones clasped hands, Ken asked, "Aren't we all supposed to hold hands?"

Phoebe had once served on a jury in a murder trial. Stan told the police where to find his wife's body, claiming he had seen it in a vision. Phoebe knew he wasn't lying, but she couldn't prove it. Only his dead wife's testimony could convince the others on the jury that he was innocent. Angela's spirit had desperately wanted to clear her husband and catch her killer. She had been easy to summon. The new ghost in the Manor might not be so anxious to cooperate. They'd have a better chance of holding it for interrogation within a circle that bound their psychic and physical energies.

"Actually," Phoebe said, "holding hands would be a good idea."

"I can't *wait* to see what you do next." Ken grinned as he gripped Piper's and O'Brien's hand. "One thing is sure: Your parties will never bore anyone to death."

"This won't work unless you take it seriously." Phoebe held Ken's gaze until he adopted a suitably sober expression. "Okay," he said.

Phoebe took Cole's hand in hers, Cole took Fiona's, and O'Brien grabbed Fiona's other hand. The circle was complete.

Drawing power from one another, the witches recited the summoning spell again.

> *Hear these words, hear our cry,*
> *Spirit from the other side,*
> *Come to us, we summon thee,*
> *Cross now the great divide.*

At the conclusion of the spell, Phoebe took over the ritual. She had gently requested Angela's presence, but she commanded the malicious ghost. "Spirit! You will appear and commune with us now!"

This time, since the ghost was already inside the Manor, the summoning incantation worked.

A bitter, cold wind blew through the room, and a dark gray cloud appeared above the candles.

"Is that smoke, or am I hallucinating?" Ken asked in a harsh whisper. He flinched when O'Brien kicked him under the table.

Fiona remained calm, but she was on edge with anticipation.

Phoebe expected the vapors to condense into the transparent form of the person the ghost had once been. Instead, the cloud hovered, then it elongated into a stream that shot toward Coop and enveloped him in a gray haze. Phoebe tensed, curbing the urge to call his name. The faint image of a man with dark hair and a mustache, wearing an old-fashioned suit, shimmered for a split second before the ghost entered Coop's body.

Phoebe surmised that the ghost wanted to confront them as a presence of substance rather than a mere reflection of its former self. To that end, he had chosen the strongest, most imposing male body as a host.

"Who are you?" Phoebe asked.

"Who are *you*?" Speaking as the ghost, Coop's voice had the hard edge of a man accustomed to being obeyed. The eyes that usually looked on Phoebe with rapt adoration narrowed with animosity.

"One of the very displeased owners of this house," Phoebe said evenly. "You're haunting it. I want to know why."

Curling Coop's lips into a sneer, the ghost stared off into the ether, mulling over the request. He spoke as though patronizing a small child. "Telling might be amusing, but it will *change* nothing. I *will* have the satisfaction to which I'm entitled."

Phoebe sensed Piper's extreme anger at the ghost. Her sister was not intimidated by the dead man's actions or his arrogance, but she bit her lip and kept quiet.

"Great job with the voice, Coop," Ken said.

"Do you mock me, sir?" The ghost turned on Ken with a pointed stare.

"Wouldn't think of it," Ken returned glibly.

"I am not a man to be crossed or taken lightly." The ghost's tone was tight with menace.

"No," Phoebe quickly interjected, trying to diffuse the clash. "You're a ghost with a story we all want to hear."

Piper cut right to the chase. "How did you die?"

"Hold your impudent tongue!" Coop's eyes flashed with the dark light of his captor's disdain. "I will tell this tale in my own good time."

Good, Phoebe thought. *I hope it takes until dawn, when the other dead guys come home.*

The ghost, however, did not mince words. "My wife had a disrespectful, rebellious nature. She often infuriated me. That's why I killed her."

No one spoke for several poignant seconds.

"And what did she do that she deserved killing?" O'Brien asked, genuinely curious.

"I instructed her to dismiss a maid, and she refused," the dead man said flatly. "That the hired girl had simply forgotten to bring sugar with my tea *was* trivial, but my wife should not have ignored my wishes in the matter."

"So you murdered her?" Phoebe asked, aghast. Hearing the horrible declaration in her husband's voice was unsettling, but it also reminded her that Coop was as good as the ghost was evil. She also realized that she was witnessing the beginning of the scenario she had seen in her premonition. Before long, the ghost possessing Coop's body would fly into a violent rage.

"Throttled the life's breath out of her with my own hands." Coop's face twisted into an ugly visage of cruelty. "Not that it rid me of the troublesome woman."

Paige looked confused. "What do you mean?"

"Within hours of her death," the ghost said, "she came back."

"A crisis apparition," Fiona exclaimed. "They're triggered by the trauma of dying and usually occur within twelve hours of the person's death," she went on to explain matter-of-factly.

"You learn something new every day," Piper muttered.

"I could not tolerate the idea of being haunted by her for the rest of my life," the ghost continued, "so I ended it."

"You killed yourself?" Ken blurted out. After realizing his implied interest, he recovered. "Great plot twist, Coop. Never saw it coming."

"My wife didn't see me coming." The ghost was too involved with the events surrounding his own demise to care about the skeptic. "Despite her occasional displays of independence, she needed me for everything in life. I convinced her she couldn't exist without me in death, either."

"And she believed you?" Fiona seemed surprised.

"Of course," he barked, eying the ghost hunter with contempt. "For one hundred years."

As an empath, Phoebe was more aware of the crushing force of the ghost's domineering personality than the others. It wasn't hard to understand how a woman raised in an age of male dominance could be cowed into believing everything her husband told her. Lost in a moment of sympathy, Phoebe was caught off guard by a jolting increase of hostility.

"Victoria was bound to Earth, and more importantly, to me, until"—the ghost pulled Coop's right hand free from Fiona's and pointed at her—"you came to our house on Nob Hill."

"Victoria?" Stunned, Fiona shrank back. "Oh, my God."

"Priceless!" Ken exclaimed.

"Don't anyone else let go!" Phoebe warned. The ghost had broken the physical circle, but he hadn't retreated. Either the power of the psychic bond was still intact, or he wasn't ready to go. Either way, she was grateful. They still didn't have enough information to neutralize or vanquish him.

"Do you know him, Fiona?" Piper asked.

Fiona nodded. "His name is Sheldon Winters."

Bursts of frigid air coursed through the room,

emanations of the ghost's intense wrath, all of it directed at the ghost hunter.

"What happened at the house on Nob Hill?" Paige asked.

"A developer was going to convert the mansion into condos," Fiona said. "A friend of mine wanted to buy in, but I talked her out of it."

"Why?" O'Brien looked up into her face.

"The mansion had changed hands almost thirty times in the previous century," Fiona said. "I explained to my friend that the original owner had murdered his wife and killed himself in 1907, and their ghosts were haunting the house."

"If those are the facts, then why are you upset with Fiona, Mr. Winters?" Phoebe asked, perplexed.

"*Victoria* heard what she said!" Sheldon ripped his other hand free from Phoebe, breaking the human chain. Everyone else around the table held on. "My wife wasn't aware that I had shot myself until Fiona told her, and that's when she knew." He wailed. "That's when she knew!"

"What?" Piper tried to shake her hair out of her eyes. "Knew what?"

"That I committed suicide. My soul was doomed." The wind whipped harder, and the timbre of Sheldon's tortured voice reverberated off the walls. "I couldn't hold her against her will. She was free to go."

"Victoria crossed over," Phoebe stated.

"Yes!" Sheldon seethed with suppressed rage. "Leaving me with two wretched choices: I could go to hell, or spend eternity alone."

Might as well be no choice, Phoebe thought with a shudder.

"Well, I have no intention of going to hell," Sheldon went on, "and I *won't* be trapped here alone."

"What do you want from us?" Piper demanded.

"Nothing!" Sheldon exploded out of his chair, knocking it over. He grabbed a ceramic witch figurine off the sideboard and threw it at the ghost hunter. "How dare you interfere with my affairs, you meddling wench!"

The scene played out exactly as Phoebe had seen it in her vision. She clung to her sisters' hands for support. It was a relief to know that Coop was only a vessel for the dead man's rampage, but Fiona was in grave danger. They now knew the ghost's name and story. That would have to be enough.

"Let go now!" As Phoebe released Piper and Paige, Ken and O'Brien dropped hands. However, the disintegration of their bound psychic energies did not affect the ghost.

Still raging in Coop's body, Sheldon pelted Fiona with everything available to him; candy and bits of plaster he scooped off the sideboard. Then he lunged across the table, screaming. "You ruined everything, and you will pay!"

"Take it easy!" Ken grabbed Coop's arm, concerned for Fiona's safety despite their differences. "This has gone far enough."

Sheldon whirled and punched Ken in the jaw, sending the professor reeling into the wall.

Piper raised her hands to freeze the room, but didn't. Her power wouldn't affect the ghost or anything in direct contact with him. Phoebe tensed. She didn't want to use her martial arts skills against her husband, but she knew Coop would gladly suffer a few bruises or even a broken bone to save an Innocent.

Fiona slipped off her chair, avoiding Sheldon's grasp. Terrified, but keeping her wits, she backed up and challenged him. *"You're* responsible for your fate, Sheldon. No one else."

"No one makes a fool of me!" Moving with superhuman speed, Sheldon clamped Fiona's neck in a vicelike grip.

Phoebe sprang forward, kicking Coop behind the knees to jar his hand loose and buckle his legs. The ghost stood firm.

Fiona clawed at Coop's hand, drawing blood, but Sheldon's grip tightened. As she started to gag, Paige reached out to orb her to safety.

But the ghost suddenly released her.

The image of Sheldon Winters was superimposed over Coop's tall frame for a second before the ghost dissipated back into the ether. In parting, he uttered a few final, despicable words.

"Fiona will spend eternity with me."

Chapter Nine

The implication of Sheldon's last words before he dissipated hit Paige hard. In order to spend eternity with the ghost, Fiona had to die.

Coop collapsed on the floor, and Phoebe rushed to his side. The possession had drained him, but he was conscious. She pressed the edge of her skirt against his hand to blot the blood from the scratches.

Piper flicked on the lights, blew out the candles, and leaned over to stare at Ken. The skeptic stared back, slightly dazed, but with no injuries worse than a swollen jaw.

Paige hurried over to Fiona, the Innocent she should have been protecting. "Are you okay?" she asked as she helped the shaken woman to a chair.

"He's going to kill me," Fiona said, her voice hoarse and her breath ragged from being choked.

"No, he's not." Paige brushed white plaster

dust off Fiona's shoulders. "We won't let him."

O'Brien's brow knit with worry. "Could I get you something, Fiona? Hot tea with a soothing dollop of honey and lemon, perhaps."

"Yes, thank you." Fiona forced a smile, then recoiled when Coop started to stand.

"It's just Coop," Paige assured her. "He won't be hurting you now."

"Now?" Coop's puzzled expression turned to one of horror when he noticed the red bruises on Fiona's neck. "Did I do that?"

"No," Phoebe said. "Sheldon Winters did. I knew you weren't a raving maniac."

"Was that ever in question?" Coop look confused as he rubbed the back of his leg.

"I, uh—had a—" Phoebe glanced at Ken. "You know, a *hunch*. I should have said something, but I didn't want to spoil the party."

"And you can see how well that worked out," Piper muttered, sighing as she scanned the debris.

"Did I black out?" Coop flexed his arms, as though trying to work off the lingering effects of the ghost's presence.

"You channeled a very bad ghost," Phoebe said.

"And took your part much too seriously." Ken stood up, testing his jaw.

"I don't remember anything," Coop said.

"You gave this blighter a bit of a thrashin', but needin' it he was." O'Brien shook his fist at

Ken as he passed on his way to the kitchen.

"You hit him," Phoebe said, clarifying for Coop. "Or rather, the ghost did."

"Forget the ghost. The joke's over." The bravado was gone from Ken's expression and tone. "You and Fiona obviously planned this whole elaborate demonstration to scare me."

"You think we wrecked our house to play a joke on someone we don't even know?" Paige blinked in disbelief.

"You're all fanatics about this supernatural stuff," Ken said. "It's not that far-fetched to think you got carried away. I'll admit, it was entertaining at first, but it's not funny anymore."

"No, it's not funny," Piper agreed. "If we don't send Sheldon Winters to the great below where he belongs, someone could die."

"Me," Fiona said.

"Thank goodness Coop expelled him before that happened," Paige said.

"I didn't do anything," Coop said. "The ghost had complete control."

Phoebe frowned. "Then why didn't he finish strangling Fiona?"

"I was starting to orb her out of danger when he let go," Paige said. "Sheldon must have known we'd use our powers to save her."

"That wasn't the reason. He didn't want to kill me here." Fiona wasn't offering a possible explanation. She sounded certain. "Sheldon's reality is anchored to the house on Nob Hill. He can't leave it."

"Except on Halloween," Piper said.

"Yes." Fiona exhaled wearily. "Apparently, he's been waiting for this night since my friend and I were at the mansion ten months ago."

"That still doesn't explain why he didn't kill you when he had the chance," Ken said. He took offense when everyone glared at him. "What? You concocted this intricate mystery for my benefit. Why shouldn't I play along?"

"This isn't a game, Ken," Fiona said. "Sheldon blames me because his wife crossed over, and he wants me to replace her. That's why he has to kill me at the mansion on Nob Hill."

"I don't get it," Ken said.

"Have you been listening to *anything* we've talked about tonight?" Paige didn't understand how an intelligent university professor could be so dense.

Ken's temper flared. "You wouldn't let me take notes!"

"He's got a point," Piper conceded.

Fiona continued. "Sheldon has to strangle me with his own hands in the mansion, just as he did his wife. Re-creating Victoria's death will keep his reality intact, and being murdered in the same house will anchor *my* spirit to him and the site."

"Then what's the problem?" Ken looked honestly bewildered. "If the ghost doesn't want to kill you here, you're safe as long as you don't leave. So just wait. According to your rules, *he* has to go home at dawn."

"But he'll be back," Phoebe said.

"Absolutely." Piper nodded. "Next Halloween."

"And the next Halloween and the next, until he gets what he wants," Phoebe went on. Being a ghost, Sheldon would still be earthbound when the leprechauns and other visiting spirits went back through Paige's portal. "Unless we get rid of the ghost. That's the only way Fiona will be safe."

"Forever." Paige sighed. "I am so sorry, Fiona. This mess is my fault. If I hadn't cast the summoning spell and opened the way between worlds—"

Fiona cut her off. "Don't be sorry, Paige! The enormous amount of spiritual activity is what drew me to the Manor."

"Setting you up so Sheldon Winters could stalk you all night," Paige said.

"Sheldon would have found me wherever I was," Fiona explained. "And he probably would have found a way to lure me back to his mansion. But I was *here*, the only place in the city where I could find help. Otherwise, I'd be facing him alone."

"With only Ken Carson for backup," Paige quipped.

"I'm not helpless," Ken objected.

Paige chose not to remind Ken that a Cupid

possessed by a ghost had flattened him with one punch.

"I'm sorry your house has taken such a beating," Fiona said.

"Yeah, well." Phoebe glanced around the room. "This won't be the first time Piper's handyman husband has had to put it back together. And it probably won't be the last."

"And I am *so* glad Leo isn't the I-told-you-so type. Yesterday, he tried to tell me I was becoming too complacent." Piper picked up the ceramic witch. The tip of the conical hat was broken off and the face was chipped. She dropped it into the rubble of broken dishes and mashed snacks. "I need a cup of tea."

"C'mon, Fiona," Paige said. "We're not leaving you alone until this is over. Sheldon will keep trying to get you out of the house."

O'Brien had cleared the kitchen table and set it with cups that survived Sheldon's tantrums in the cupboard. A pot of tea steeped beside a creamer, a bowl of sugar, and a plate of broken cookies.

"You didn't get these off the floor, did you?" Ken poked at half a sugar cookie with orange icing.

"Lookin' for another thrashin', are ya?" The leprechaun huffed and banged a cookie tin on the table. "They were in here, if you must know. Cider's in the cold box."

Ken ate the cookie.

"Sheldon just expended a lot of energy, but he'll strike again as soon as he gets his strength back." Sitting down, Phoebe poured a cup of tea and did some quick calculations. Since they had evacuated the house two hours before, the ghost had recharged twice—before the earthquake attack and again before the séance. "His get-out-of-your-haunt-free-on-Halloween window gets smaller every minute that goes by."

Piper pulled the cider out of the fridge. "We know his name and the year he died. It shouldn't be too hard to find his grave."

"You and Phoebe do the research. I'll get started on the . . . cure." Paige hesitated to say "potion." They had been talking freely, but that was before Sheldon had interacted with them. Despite Fiona's assurances that the ghost's perceptions were limited to his original existence, he knew more about them now. She'd rather talk in code than risk tipping him off. Leaving to retrieve the Book of Shadows from the dining room, she turned back when Phoebe called.

"I left my laptop upstairs in Piper's room," Phoebe said. "Will you get it? I can check the county burial records online."

"You brought your computer to a party?" Paige took her cell phone everywhere, but she didn't mind leaving the World Wide Web at home.

"I'm thinking about writing a book," Phoebe said, "and I have brainstorms at the oddest times. I don't want to forget anything before I have a chance to write it down. So . . . I keep the laptop handy."

"Paper and pencil are so hard to find these days," Piper teased as Paige orbed out.

While they waited for Paige, Piper sipped her tea and absently listened to Ken and O'Brien's insulting banter. She tried not to worry about her demolished kitchen, but it was impossible not to calculate the losses. The floor was littered with small, mostly replaceable items Sheldon had flung off the counters and shelves: trash, boxes and cans, cookbooks, knickknacks, baking products, china, glassware. As far as she could tell, the appliances and furniture were splattered with buffet leftovers but not damaged. She had taken great pains to clean up as she cooked so the kitchen would be presentable during the open house. Sheldon's mess would take days to remove, and she couldn't help feeling discouraged.

Paige walked in from the dining room, having orbed back downstairs where Ken couldn't see. It was hard to believe, but so far the professor had found ways to explain everything he had seen, heard, and felt. His capacity for self-delusion was remarkable.

"I see Sheldon's still lying low." Paige handed Phoebe her laptop carry case, dropped the Book of Shadows on the center island, and started moving food containers to the counters.

"For the moment," Piper said.

"What if you can't find the grave?" Ken held out a cup for Piper to pour more cider. "What do you do then? Burn down his old house on Nob Hill?"

The overhead lights flickered.

"Why would we do that?" Coop frowned at the professor.

"Well," Ken said, "we don't have a dead guy to read the spell in the phantom zone—"

"The ghostly plane," Piper corrected.

"Seamus and the other lads might return early," O'Brien pointed out.

"And they might not," Ken said. "So if you don't know where Sheldon is buried, the only option left is to remove whatever he's obsessed with." He shot Paige a smug look of satisfaction. "I didn't forget *everything* you discussed."

"Five gold stars—except Sheldon isn't obsessed with his mansion," Paige said. "He was obsessed with his wife. And now, Fiona."

"We've been in this situation before." Phoebe leaned forward, hands on her teacup. "Martha Van Lewen was haunted by the ghost of Elias Lundy, a lovesick chauffer she shot. She killed herself so his ghost wouldn't kill her grandson."

"Did it work?" Ken asked.

"Perfectly. The minute Martha died, Elias went *poof!*" Piper flicked her fingers.

"It was more like he turned into a flaming

torch and went straight to hell," Phoebe said.

"But Fiona's destruction is not an option," Coop stated for the record.

"So we're brewing a mandrake root—"

"Tea!" Paige yelled out as she pulled a small caldron from a lower cupboard and set it on the burner.

"Right! More tea." Piper realized that it probably wasn't wise to let Sheldon know they were making a potion. "Just what we need to calm our nerves," she added for good measure.

Phoebe took her laptop and a power cord out of the case. After attaching the cord to the computer, she plugged it into the wall socket.

The lights crackled and went out.

Ken snapped on a small halogen flashlight. "I carry one whenever I follow Fiona because she's always traipsing through graveyards and abandoned buildings. I've twisted my ankle in holes I didn't see way too many times."

"You couldn't see the holes because they weren't there until you put your foot down," Fiona said. "The spirits made them where you were walking. It's one of their favorite ways to harass skeptics."

"I could do with more holes and less demolition," Piper said wryly.

Phoebe flipped open the laptop and hit the power button. The screen stayed dark until she removed the electrical cord and switched to battery power. Once activated, the screen was an eerie source of light in the darkness.

"Is the power out in the whole house or just this room?" Paige asked.

"I'll see." As Coop stood up to leave, Piper opened a drawer in the small hutch behind her. She pulled out two flashlights and gave him one. He aimed the beam at the dining room door. "Be right back."

"I'll help you." O'Brien hurried out after him.

"Lock the doors and windows while you're out there!" Phoebe hollered, then lowered her voice to explain. "Sheldon wants to get Fiona out. Why make it easy?"

"I don't think he'll have a problem upgrading his huff-and-puff to blow the doors and windows out of their frames." Paige abruptly shifted gears. "Could you bring that flashlight over here, Piper? I do *not* want to mix the wrong ingredients."

"Heaven forbid." Piper flicked on the other flashlight and went to hold it for her sister. They had enough trouble without adding more magical mayhem.

"How did Sheldon know to shut off the electricity?" Phoebe asked Fiona. "Weren't most people still using oil lamps in 1907?"

"Most people were," Fiona said. "But Sheldon was rich. Part of his mansion was wired."

"Then we can be glad they didn't have computers," Phoebe said, typing something into hers. "It might help if we knew more about him, to narrow down the search for his grave."

"The Hollow Hill website has a pretty good file on the Winters mansion," Fiona suggested. "I did a lot of research before I told my friend about the haunting."

"Fran mentioned that site," Paige said. "Will you get the powdered dragon's blood, Piper? We need to cut down the boil time on this baby."

Ken grimaced. "She's not using real blood?"

"It's a tree resin," Piper said. "Very potent."

"And Sheldon Winters was *very* rich." Phoebe turned the laptop so Fiona and Ken could see the screen.

Piper handed Paige the dragon's blood, then found the battery-powered emergency lantern Leo kept in the cabinet under the sink. She turned it on for Paige and went back to the table.

The website file included a photograph of Sheldon and Victoria Winters. Mrs. Winters, a slim, elegant lady with sad eyes, had been several years younger than her middle-aged husband. Sheldon had dark wavy hair parted on the side, bushy eyebrows, and a thick mustache. He stood with a walking cane and wore a gray herringbone coat and vest, a high-collar shirt and knotted tie, spats, and striped trousers. The lines of a stern, unyielding scowl were etched in his face.

"Sheldon and Victoria survived the big earthquake in 1906," Phoebe said. "With minimal damage to the mansion. They died almost exactly a year later."

"Better hurry before he figures out what we're up to," Piper cautioned. "He may be set in his own reality, but he saw ours through Coop's eyes."

"Could that alter his perceptions?" Phoebe asked as she did a keyword search for county burial records.

"Anything is possible," Fiona said, "but I have no idea what to expect."

"Then we'd better be ready for the worst," Piper said.

"Here we go." Phoebe clicked a link. A comprehensive website with information on deaths and burials in San Francisco County dating back to the late 1800s came up. She clicked on the first decade of the twentieth century, then on 1907, and then on the appropriate alphabetical designation.

"There it is." Piper pointed to the double listing for Sheldon and his wife. The table began to shake as Phoebe moved the cursor. "Hurry . . . ," Piper cautioned.

Phoebe clicked on the Winters link, then lifted the compact computer off the table. The table stopped thumping.

Piper held her breath. Sheldon was a quick study, and despite Phoebe's high-speed wireless modem, it seemed to take forever for the information to load.

"Got it." Phoebe's eyes flicked over the screen. "Nob Hill Gardens Cemetery, plot—" Her chair was suddenly pulled out from under her.

Piper, Fiona, and Ken all reached to save Phoebe from a painful landing. The laptop fell to the floor. When the table flipped onto its side, Ken dragged Phoebe's legs clear. The edge of the heavy table crushed the computer.

"My laptop!" Pale with shock, Phoebe stared at the shattered machine. "He killed my laptop!"

A stream of cold air raced through the kitchen, a ghostly victory lap that stirred the litter on the floor and shook the light fixtures.

"Was all your work on it?" Paige asked.

"No." Phoebe picked up the broken pieces when Ken lifted the table. "I've got everything backed up—at the office and at home. I just really liked this computer."

"My herbal *tea* will make you feel better." Paige spoke in the stilted voice of an amateur actress. Her reference to "tea" was designed to hide the nature of the potion and their intent from the ghost. "But it has to brew for forty-five minutes. Roughly."

Piper used the flashlight to find the pad and pen Phoebe had left on the table. She jotted a note and showed it to Phoebe: Telephone Dad?

"Worth a shot," Phoebe said.

Our best shot right now, Piper thought. Their father had a computer and no ghost to smash it before he could get the exact location of Sheldon's grave. Besides, it had been almost three hours since Leo had left with the kids, and she wanted to check on them.

"Why don't you see if you can find the pieces of that message?" Piper mimicked Paige's bad acting voice and pointed to the broken laptop. Sheldon had deduced that they used the device as a source of information, but she doubted he knew the computer was now completely useless. In his time, a torn note could be pieced together. Even a burned scrap of paper might yield a vital word or two.

"Are you kidding?" Ken asked. "That laptop is toast—"

Piper nudged him with her elbow, hard. The Charmed Ones would have been toast long ago if they were as slow on the uptake as the academic. She spoke with deliberate care. "The hard drive is okay, and that's where *all* the information is *stored*."

"They didn't have computers in 1907." Whispering, Fiona spoke so fast, her words were almost unintelligible.

Her meaning was lost on Ken. He just rolled his eyes and threw up his hands. "This is getting really old, really fast. I'm done."

"Then sit down and shut up. Please." Piper picked up the cordless phone. Hoping Fiona and Phoebe could distract Sheldon with the laptop, she eased into the dining room and speed-dialed her dad. "Hey! How's it going?"

"Piper?" Victor sounded uncertain. "There's so much static on the line, I can hardly hear you."

There hadn't been *any* static when Piper used the phone earlier. Of course, Alexander Graham Bell had invented the telephone in 1876. Sheldon was probably rich enough to have had a telephone, too.

"I don't have much time." Piper didn't wait for Victor to respond. "You have to find the exact location of a grave in Nob Hill Gardens Cemetery—"

The line went dead.

Sheldon ripped the Happy Halloween banner off the window, wrapped the strung-together letters around the phone, and yanked it from her grasp. Piper tensed, expecting another attack, but the ghost moved on.

Piper hurried through the sunroom into the living room. Coop and O'Brien were struggling to close a front window. "What's going on?" she asked as she picked up the extension. There was no dial tone.

Coop stepped back. "We tried, but we can't get this window closed. Sheldon obviously wants to keep an exit available."

"At least we know about it so we can keep Fiona away from it," Piper said as they headed back to the kitchen. She had to guess what Sheldon knew.

The ghost obviously felt threatened because they were trying to locate his grave. But did he know why? They might find another way to contact Victor, but the effort would be pointless if Sheldon understood the plan. However, if the ghost had no interest in Paige's herbal *tea*, it was safe to assume he hadn't connected the potion with the grave and his ultimate demise.

Back in the kitchen, O'Brien scurried about locking the door and windows. The potion simmered untouched on the burner. Paige was back at the table with Phoebe, Fiona, and Ken, eating cookies and drinking cider.

"Any luck, Phoebe?" Piper asked as though she had actually expected her sister to find a fragment of a message.

"No, sorry." Phoebe casually tossed the computer into a pile of trash and held her hand out to clasp Coop's. "You?"

"Nope," Piper said. "I got as far as telling Dad the name of the cemetery before I was cut off. There's no dial tone in the living room, either."

"So he severed all your *land* lines," Fiona said pointedly.

Everyone understood what Fiona was getting at except Ken.

"That's no problem." Ken reached into his pocket. "You can use my—"

Piper froze the professor before he mentioned his cell phone. Sheldon would instantly deduce the function of the compact phone, and he would just as quickly destroy every one they tried to use. However, she was absolutely certain he had no concept of a text message.

Phoebe put her hand over Ken's mouth, muffling the end of his sentence when the freeze wore off. "Do not say a word." Her eyes flashed a warning. "Not one word. Understand?"

Ken nodded vigorously and batted her hand away.

By Piper's calculations, assuming Fiona also carried a cell phone, there were five in the house. The odds were better than even that she or one of her sisters could send a text message without the ghost knowing. They would each send the necessary information to Henry, Leo, and Victor, improving their chances of getting through even more. And they'd have Fiona's and Ken's phones for backup if their phones were destroyed. Piper slipped back into bad-actor voice. "It's too bad we can't *talk* to Henry, Leo, and Victor. I hope they don't forget to *read*."

Coop frowned but didn't comment. He was still adapting to the secret-sister meanings hidden in many of their conversations.

Paige and Phoebe exchanged a puzzled glance.

Paige brightened first. "Oh, yeah. It would be a shame if Wyatt and Chris didn't get the *message* you sent."

When Phoebe still didn't get it, Fiona jumped

in. "It won't be long before the boys are reading Ken's *text*books."

"I've written two," Ken said.

"Oh, gosh." Phoebe winced, but she refrained from slapping her forehead when the meaning of the coded message became clear.

Piper's cell phone was in her purse. Normally, her purse was lying on a counter in the kitchen or hanging in the hall. Tonight, because of the party, she had taken it to the bedroom. Phoebe and Paige had left their belongings upstairs for the same reason.

"I've got a splitting headache," Piper said. "There's some *aspirin* in my purse on my bed. Would you mind going upstairs again, Paige?"

"Of course not." Paige looked at Phoebe. Phoebe nodded. "Be back in a jiffy."

As Paige orbed out, Fiona jumped up. "My chair just got hot."

When the seat burst into flames, Paige aborted her departure. Everyone else around the table stood up.

"Are my pants scorched?" Ken pulled at the fabric behind him.

Coop gingerly touched his chair. "Not hot."

"Neither is mine," Phoebe said.

Fiona began shifting from one foot to the other. "The floor's heating up. It feels like my shoes are on fire!" Around her, the floor began to glow orange, then red, as the temperature rose.

"Jump, Fiona!" Piper yelled. The ghost hunter

didn't hesitate. Piper froze her the instant her feet left the superheated floor.

"You can't keep her suspended for long," Phoebe said. "The minute everything speeds up, she'll burn her feet on the floor."

"Paige!" Piper yelled.

Before the Whitelighter could orb Fiona, the invisible arms of Sheldon Winters grabbed her. She awakened from Piper's freeze the instant the ghost touched her. As she was swept through the dining room, she grabbed the chandelier and pulled free of the ghost's grasp. Paige orbed her back into the group, and the floor began heating up again as soon as she touched down.

"It's too hot." Fiona backed toward the dining room to escape floor temperatures that rose wherever she stepped. The effect was similar to the spirit holes that had appeared for the sole purpose of tripping Ken. The floor cooled behind Fiona as Sheldon herded her toward the front of the house.

When Piper tried to follow, a white-hot ring of flooring three feet wide formed around her and the others.

"I want to leave now." Sweat ran down Ken's face, and the leather in his shoes began to smoke. "I'm not going to stand here and burn alive." Panicking, he crouched to try jumping the fiery ring. He collapsed instead.

O'Brien bent over the fallen man. "He fainted."

"Great," Piper said. Her relief was twofold: The man was okay, and he couldn't annoy them while he was out cold.

"The tea will evaporate in this heat," Paige said.

"You can't vanquish Sheldon without it," Coop said. "Orb O'Brien and Ken somewhere safe and put me by the sink. I'll use water to dampen the heat while you go after Fiona."

"Stay away from the windows and doors, Fiona!" Piper shouted as Paige orbed the men to the far side of the kitchen.

"Please don't let us be too late," Paige muttered as she orbed her sisters. When they materialized in front of the open living room window, Fiona was halfway across the room, zigzagging to slow down her advance.

As the Charmed Ones started toward her, the room filled with a blinding cloud of dust and debris.

"I can't see her!" Paige shouted.

Phoebe stood by the window, blocking it with her outstretched arms. "She hasn't come this way."

"Fiona!" Piper screamed the woman's name, but there was no response. When the dust settled, Phoebe's greatest fear was confirmed. The ghost hunter was gone.

Chapter Ten

Grady couldn't remember a Samhain when he had had more fun. "These modern Americans know how to celebrate All Hallows' Eve, that's for sure."

"Are you daft, Grady? Not a one has offered us a pint or a haunch of meat," Connor complained.

"And they don't light a village bonfire," Marty said. "Samhain just isn't the same without a bonfire."

"But they're very generous with sweets." Seamus peered into his tam. He carried the hat upside down, and it was overflowing with candy.

"Mostly," Liam agreed. "I wasn't so pleased with those that slammed doors in our faces. What's wrong with bein' old, I'd like to know."

"Aye." Grady nodded solemnly, then burst into a gleeful laugh. "But the ounce o' bad luck we gave back made the insult worth it."

"It's truly amazing how much can go wrong in five minutes." Marty slapped his knee. "Porch lights burning out and screen doors fallin' off the hinges."

"Sneezin' and hands bustin' out in warts," Liam said.

"Bah." Connor paused to shake a stone out of his shoe. "A few smashed jack-o'-lanterns and minor maladies weren't price enough for disrespectin' their elders."

"True as that may be, O'Brien promised the Charmed Ones we'd be on our best behavior." Seamus unwrapped a soft pink square labeled "bubble gum" and popped it into his mouth.

"And we might as well be gettin' back," Marty said. "The streets are all deserted, and no candles light the windows."

"Then beware of lost sprits that can't find their way," Connor said as he started walking.

"We're not the only ones still roamin' the night with the ghosts." Grady pointed down the block. A man was trying to force a boy to come along with him. "Let's see what that's about."

The leprechauns moved into the shadows and stayed hidden behind a hedge as they crept forward. Grady didn't take kindly to big people picking on smaller ones. This, however, turned out to be a father trying to deal with a disobedient son who was intent on running away.

"What's going on, Barry?" The man grabbed the boy's arm. "Where are you going?"

"I don't know!" The boy wailed and tried to pull free. "The pants are doing it!"

"The pants?" The man took the boy by the shoulders and made him sit down on the sidewalk. He paused for a moment, as though trying to dispel his exasperation so he wouldn't lose his temper. "What about the pants?"

"I found them in our yard," the boy whimpered. "I tried them on before I went to bed, and they made me run out the door."

"The pants made you run?" The man asked.

"Uh-huh." The sniffling boy nodded.

"Well, we can fix that," the man said gently. "Let's just take them off."

The boy didn't argue as his father slipped the camouflage sweatpants off his legs. Leaving the pants in a heap on the sidewalk, they walked off hand in hand.

A simple solution, Grady thought, happy that the father had been so kind and understanding.

"I don't see anything strange about these knickers." Liam picked up the pants and examined them closely. "They look comfortable."

"I've seen several young boys wearing that green-and-black pattern tonight," Marty said as Liam kicked off his boots and stepped into the pants.

"I wouldn't be doin' that—" Grady's words of caution were spoken too late.

"Oh, fiddle and shamrock," Liam exclaimed, grabbing his boots as he took off running.

"And where would he be goin' so fast in his stocking feet?" Connor asked.

"Wherever the pants would be takin' him," Grady said as he and the other three leprechauns gave chase.

"Where did she go?" Phoebe tried not to panic. Except for fighting demons and almost being killed every week for eight years, losing Innocents was the worst thing that could happen.

"Did she get by you?" Piper asked, glancing at the open front window.

"No. Absolutely not," Phoebe said. She closed her eyes, but all she felt was residual, fading fear. "Do we have something that belongs to her? Maybe I can get a vision."

Paige didn't waste time talking. She orbed out and back with Fiona's forest-green cape.

Phoebe clutched the garment to her chest. Her impressions were a jumble of emotions and images:

Flashes of the attic . . . terror and overwhelming anger . . . Fiona tumbling off the roof . . .

"The attic," Phoebe said. "Fiona's on the roof—or she soon will be."

Paige orbed the sisters to the center of their magical operations.

There was no sign of Fiona, but Sheldon was having a tornado tantrum. A whirling funnel of wind tore across the floor, then leaped to the rafters, toppling boxes and blowing pictures, belts, shoulder bags, and other treasures from their hooks on the walls.

"Knock it off, Sheldon!" Piper yelled.

Phoebe ran to the open window, her heart in her throat. Fiona was standing on the roof with her arms out, fighting to keep her balance. "What are you doing, Fiona? Come back in here!"

"No!" Fiona shook her head. "He won't touch me out here. It's the only way I can have the upper hand."

Phoebe stared at the ghost hunter.

"What does that mean?" Piper ducked to avoid being bonked on the head with four volumes of an old *World Book* encyclopedia.

"She wants Sheldon to think she's going to jump," Phoebe said softly.

"Why?" Piper ran to the window with Paige close behind.

"Because if she dies here, the ghost loses," Phoebe explained. "To keep his new reality as similar to his original reality as possible, he has to strangle Fiona at the mansion so she'll be stuck there to haunt it with him. That won't happen if she kills herself by jumping off the Manor roof."

"Brilliant," Paige said. Then she frowned. "I think."

"You don't think she'd really do it, do you?" Piper asked.

"No," Phoebe said, making an educated guess

about the psychic woman's state of mind and motives. "It was the only thing she could think of to keep Sheldon at bay. She's also given us a bargaining chip and bought us some time."

Piper nodded. "Let's hope it's long enough for Paige's herbal tea to finish brewing."

Phoebe looked at Paige pointedly. "Did you get the *aspirin* from Piper's bedroom before we called you back? We still have a *big* headache."

"No problem." Paige held Phoebe's gaze as she patted her hip. "I have one right here."

"Take it when you can," Piper said.

Paige nodded, indicating she would send a text message when the opportunity arose.

"Hang on, Fiona!" Piper called out.

"Bats!" Phoebe squealed as Sheldon's raging spirit disturbed a small colony of the nocturnal creatures. Leo was diligent about finding the occasional interlopers, and Paige always orbed them into cat carriers for relocation to more bat-friendly territory. These six had moved in recently.

"I hate bats!" Piper cringed as the bats flew out the window with a great beating of wings.

"Bats are cute compared to vampires," Paige muttered as she crouched behind a stack of quilts. She pulled out her cell phone and began to punch buttons.

The bats were visible in the light of the waning harvest moon. Fiona tried to squat down as they passed over her head, and slipped. She began to slide down the slanted roof. "I'm falling off!"

Sheldon's horrified moan echoed off the wooden walls.

Piper froze Fiona, then turned to confront the ghost. "I won't save Fiona unless you go away."

The brutal gale died down to a whisper of wind, as though Sheldon were thinking things through.

Phoebe kept an eye on Fiona so she could alert Piper or Paige the instant the freeze wore off. Piper knew that even if the ghost left, it wouldn't stay away. Sheldon would never abandon his goal. They just needed a few minutes for Paige to complete the text message and orb Fiona back inside. Then, when all their other preparations were finished, they would let the ghost drive her out of the Manor.

Piper checked her watch. "You've got about two seconds before—"

The attic door slammed closed.

"Sent," Paige said, pocketing the cell phone. She stood up and orbed Fiona a split second after she tumbled off the roof.

Leo heard a faint beep and checked his cell phone. He had been anxiously waiting to hear from the Manor since they arrived at Victor's apartment, but he had no missed calls or new messages. "Is that your phone, Victor?"

"Don't think so." Victor sat on the couch reading a Halloween book with Wyatt.

"'Poor Jack, he can't go back'!" Wyatt knew the book by heart.

Victor finished the sentence: "'To the pumpkin patch ever again.'"

Chris was in his port-a-crib, watching cable cartoons with the sound turned down.

Leo couldn't believe both kids were still awake. It was just after midnight.

"It's mine." Henry flipped open his phone. "Text message from Paige."

Leo leaned forward expectantly, then turned toward the sound of a frantic knock at the door.

Victor set the book aside and went to open the door. "What do you want?" Leo heard him ask.

"It's not us that would be wantin' anything except to rid ourselves of these troublesome pants!" Seamus entered with a hat full of candy under his arm and quickly moved aside.

Liam followed him through the door, with the other leprechauns close behind. Red-faced with exertion, Liam dug in his heels to stop, but his feet propelled him to the sofa. He climbed up next to Wyatt and peeled off a pair of camouflage sweatpants.

"My pants!" Wyatt exclaimed. "They came back!"

"Your pants? Are you sure?" Leo asked. Just

before the party started, Piper had admitted she'd given Wyatt's favorite sweats to the firemen's clothing drive. It seemed highly unlikely that these were the same pair.

Wyatt looked at the tag. "Yep. They're mine." He turned the tag to show the WMH his mother had written in black ink. The initials, which stood for Wyatt Matthew Halliwell, were the recommended ID marking at his preschool. "My talk spell worked!"

"Your talk spell?" Victor asked.

"With words, like Mommy's," Wyatt said. "I told my pants to come back. And they did!"

"I'm thinkin' those pants had quite an adventure tonight," Grady said.

"And everyone that wore them too," Liam added, wiping his brow.

Leo just stared at his son. Wyatt's wish magic had been difficult to deal with for years. They never knew when he was going to animate a toy, miniaturize his parents, or unleash a TV dragon to set the city on fire. This was advanced spell casting by comparison.

Wyatt slid off the sofa and gave the pants to Chris. "These don't fit me anymore. I want you to have them."

"Pant!" Chris curled up holding the pants and went right to sleep.

Victor stared at the sleeping toddler, stunned. "Do *not* lose those pants."

"Don't worry," Leo assured him. Getting

Chris to sleep could be harder than getting an Elder to laugh.

"Do you understand this?" Henry handed Leo the cell phone. The message was short, but Leo knew what it meant.

Sheldon Winters
Nob Hill Gardens Cemetery
Died May 1907
Find, dig grave

"They've identified the ghost," Leo said. "And they want us to find the grave and dig up his coffin."

"They want us to do what?" Victor took the cell phone and read the message. "Why?"

"Short of someone dying, pouring a potion over a ghost's bones is the only way to vanquish it," Leo explained. "They wouldn't ask if it weren't necessary. Do you have a shovel?"

Victor shook his head. "I moved into an apartment so I wouldn't need one."

"Let's take my car," Henry said. "I've got a shovel and a spade in the trunk."

"Just in case you have to dig up a grave?" Victor asked with a trace of sarcasm.

"Just in case of anything," Henry said. "I've got rope, wire cutters, skeleton keys, and a bunch of other tools and supplies. When you're married to a witch, you never know what you might need."

"Smart man," Victor said, sighing.

"What about the kids?" Leo glanced back. Wyatt had climbed back onto the sofa, and Liam was reading to him.

"We can watch the wee ones," Grady said. "They'll behave, or no more rainbow rides."

"Maybe Wyatt can show me the trick to eatin' this candy." Seamus took a wad of pink gum out of his mouth. "No amount o' chewing grinds it up enough to swallow."

"Bubbles!" Wyatt took a fresh piece out of the leprechaun's hat, chewed rigorously, and blew a bubble."

"Would you look at that, now!" Seamus laughed. "It's a candy balloon!"

The bubble popped, spreading a thin layer of sticky gum over the lower half of Wyatt's face. He pulled most of it off, but small bits stuck to his skin.

"That's why I said no gum, Wyatt," Victor chided the boy as he went into the small kitchen.

"Is your computer on?" Henry asked. "I can probably get a plot number and a map from city records."

"In the bedroom." Victor hurried back in and handed Leo the wet washcloth. "Have fun, Dad."

"Aren't you supposed to use peanut butter?" Leo asked.

"That's for hair." Victor smiled. "Discovered that little trick when Piper was four. She fussed so much about smelling like a sandwich, we finally just cut the gum out."

Leo smiled. With all the kids and grandkids in their future, he'd probably need to know that someday.

"Yuck!" Wyatt wiggled as Leo cleaned his chin.

"Got it." Henry hurried out of the bedroom, stuffing a folded sheet of paper into his pocket. "Let's get moving."

Victor glanced down at his skeleton sweatshirt. "I'm dressed for this, but I wasn't planning to spend my retirement behind bars as a convicted grave robber."

"We don't usually cut it that close," Paige told Fiona when they returned to the kitchen. She had saved the woman from death-by-impact with no time to spare.

"I didn't hit the ground," Fiona said. "That's all that counts."

"Thank me lucky stars for that," O'Brien said. He held a damp cloth to Ken's forehead. The professor was still passed out on the floor.

Piper unscrewed the top of a one-quart canning jar and searched the utensil drawer. "Please tell me we have a clean ladle."

"How much of that *tea* do we need?" Paige hadn't been around the last time the Charmed Ones had tried to destroy a ghost's bones. Normally, they put potions in small vials.

"This much." Piper held up the jar then began spooning the light brown mandrake root mixture into it. She glanced around as though worried that Sheldon was spying.

The ghost had been relatively quiet since fleeing the attic. Rustling curtains and fluttering papers were the only signs that he was still in the Manor. *Taking it easy to build up his strength.* Paige glanced at the black circle on the floor. The charred area was still wet from the water Coop had used to douse the fire. The bottoms of Ken's shoes were burnt.

Paige smiled at Fiona. "I have a feeling you won't have to worry about Ken following you around on Halloween any more."

"I don't think she'll be pinin' away about that," O'Brien said.

"No, I won't," Fiona said, "but I'll miss you, O'Brien."

"Will you, now?" The leprechaun grinned broadly. "That's not a problem then. I'm not dead."

If that bit of news dismayed the ghost hunter, she didn't show it. "What happens now?" Fiona asked.

"If we want to get this done right, we'll need your help," Phoebe told her. "You have to go to the mansion. Nothing else will focus Sheldon's attention."

The windows and doors at the front of the Manor banged open and closed, evidence of the ghost's growing impatience. In his absence from the kitchen, Phoebe drove the point home to Fiona.

"We mentioned Elias Lundy before," Phoebe went on. "When he caught us digging up his grave, he drove his bones deep underground so we couldn't find them. No bones, no vanquish."

Paige gripped Fiona's shoulder. "We know it's a lot to ask, but you're the only thing that can keep him from sensing what we're doing."

"You won't be alone," Phoebe added. "Coop is going with you."

"Is that a good idea?" Fiona asked nervously.

"You mean, can the ghost possess him again?" Paige shrugged. "I honestly don't know."

Fiona nodded. "It just seems risky."

"I don't know what Sheldon is capable of," Phoebe said softly, "but I can guarantee that Coop would *never* let anything hurt you."

"No, I wouldn't." Coop placed a kitchen knife in Fiona's hand. "If something goes wrong, use this."

Fiona gasped. "I couldn't—"

"Believe me, Fiona"—Coop's gaze was earnest—"if Sheldon puts *my* hands around your neck, it's because I couldn't fight him off. You'll have no choice."

"But I'm sure it won't come to that." Phoebe smiled bravely. "Coop really is a Cupid, and he has his own resources. He couldn't live with

himself if an Innocent suffered because he failed.
It's that simple."

"Okay." Fiona took a deep breath. "Sheldon
said he had no intention of being alone or going
to hell. Well, I have no intention of living in
dread of *him* the rest of my life. I'll do whatever
needs to be done. For me *and* Victoria."

"We didn't doubt that for a minute," Phoebe
said.

"There's one more thing you'll need." Piper
opened the kitchen junk drawer and rummaged
through the odds and ends that had been collect-
ing for years. She pulled out two feathers, a
sprig of dried mistletoe, and a leather thong
from an old cat toy. Kit, their Siamese cat, had
been given human form after years of exemplary
service and didn't need the toy anymore. After
tying the feathers and mistletoe together, she
tied the other end of the thing to a chopstick and
handed it to Fiona.

"What's thus?" Fiona asked.

"A talisman," Piper said, shifting into the
loud this-is-for-the-ghost speaking mode she
and Paige had established. "Whip the charm
back and forth as you walk through the house,
and chant the spell over and over."

Paige instantly understood. Sheldon was fix-
ated, but intelligent. He'd suspect something
was amiss if they let the ghost hunter leave the
Manor without trying to stop her. Piper's impro-
vised talisman was a prop for the cover story.

Assuming the ghost had overheard them discussing their options, the sisters had concocted a
bogus spell and ritual as a decoy. They also
devised the ruse that only Fiona—as the object
of his obsession—could vanquish him. Sheldon
would easily discern that the spell wouldn't
work, but they were sure he'd attribute that to
their magical ineptness. His low regard for
women and superior attitude toward everyone
would be his undoing.

Fiona warily eyed the talisman. "For how
long?"

Until the fires of hell consume him, Paige
thought.

"You'll know," Phoebe said, pushing back
her chair. "I guess there's no point putting this
off—"

Before Phoebe could finish her sentence,
Sheldon's ghostly presence shoved Fiona toward
the dining room door. Coop took her elbow and
steered her into the hall.

Paige wanted to go with them, but the Power
of Three was needed at the grave site.

They took Fiona's car. Coop was learning to
drive so he could blend into Phoebe's nonmagi-
cal life, but he hadn't quite mastered the art of
navigating city streets. If Sheldon should man-
age to possess him again, the ghost would have
no experience behind the wheel. Fiona also knew
the way to the ghost's mansion.

"Is he here?" Fiona asked, stopping at a red light. "In the car with us?"

Lying was against Coop's code of conduct, so it was difficult to fib effectively, even for a good reason. But he didn't want to frighten Fiona unnecessarily, either. He sensed the ghost was nearby, but so far, Sheldon seemed content to just ride along.

"I'm sure he's tracking us," Coop fudged, "but he won't do anything to harm you out here."

Fiona smiled. "You sound positive."

"I am," Coop said, smiling back. "He won't try anything until we're at the mansion."

"Then maybe I should take the long way around." Fiona put on her turn signal.

Sheldon's wrath cut through Coop like icy fingers.

"Not a good idea," Coop said. "Just go slow. We don't want to get killed in an accident." The pressure eased and he sought to distract Fiona with more pleasant conversation. "You were very kind to O'Brien tonight."

"He's sweet," Fiona said.

"For a smitten leprechaun," Coop agreed, "but he's not your type."

Fiona looked at him askance. "How would you know my type?"

"I'm a Cupid. It's my business to know." Coop didn't hide a sly grin. "The right man will come along—soon."

Fiona winced. "Please, don't tell me it's Ken!"

"It's not Ken." Coop laughed. "There's a perfect match for everyone, but finding the professor's ideal mate would be quite a challenge."

They rode the rest of the way in relative silence. Discussing Fiona's ghost-hunting experiences seemed ill advised, and Sheldon became more threatening as they neared his old Nob Hill home. Twice he tried to enter Coop's body, once as a piercing stream and again using the tactics of an amoeba engulfing its prey. Coop repelled both attempts with the power of his will.

When Fiona turned into the drive that lead up to the house, Sheldon hit Coop with the full force of his obsessive rage and desire.

Coop stiffened, his lungs and throat constricting as the vengeful spirit of Sheldon Winters invaded his body.

Chapter Eleven

Coop struggled against the dark oblivion that had shrouded his consciousness the first time Sheldon Winters took possession of him. Being swamped by the ghost's oppressive personality felt like drowning, but he couldn't allow Sheldon to overwhelm and suppress him. More than Fiona's life was at stake; her eternal existence was in jeopardy.

The ghost's presence neutralized Coop's Cupid powers. To compensate, Coop visualized his essence as a thin spike with a needle-sharp point. Concentrating his mental energies, he slid the spike slowly through the black pitch of evil that cut him off from the world. When he was aware of his surroundings again, he became a phantom of himself. Hiding within his own body, he waited for the right moment to evict the vile spirit.

"You can leave the vehicle anywhere," Sheldon said, concealing his identity from Fiona. "Here is good."

"We can't block other people's cars," Fiona said. "What if someone wants to leave?"

The question annoyed the ghost. "That would be inconvenient."

Fiona laughed. "I guess you really don't know much about driving."

"I'm just anxious to finish this," Sheldon said.

"Me, too." Fiona pulled into an empty space, turned off the engine, and removed the key. "It looks like three of the condos are occupied."

Coop extended a tendril of his true self to test the ghost's resistance. Sheldon was tense with anticipation and a measure of trepidation. His goal—Fiona's murder—was within reach, but he hadn't achieved it yet. Expelling the intruder would be easier when Sheldon was certain of success and relaxed his vigilance.

"We can get into the vacant rooms," the ghost said, pointing to a darkened downstairs corner. "I can open a window."

Fiona slid out of the car but hung back as Sheldon started toward the house. "Maybe we should wait a few minutes, until we're, uh, sure no one sees us trying to break in."

Coop wasn't surprised that Fiona was balking. For her, going into the mansion was the same as going to her own execution.

"You can't do the ritual out here," Sheldon reminded her.

"I know, but it's not like—" Fiona caught

herself before she revealed that the spell wouldn't work.

Nice one, Coop thought. Although she didn't know Sheldon was occupying his body, she realized that the ghost was probably close by.

"A few more minutes won't matter," Fiona insisted.

Sheldon held out Coop's hand. "Come with me. Everything will be fine."

Coop hoped Fiona would keep stalling. Every second gave Phoebe and her sisters a bit longer to work their magic. But the ghost hunter gave in, taking his hand and slinking through the night. In his eagerness, Sheldon went directly to a window that wasn't locked.

"That's odd." A tremor shook Fiona's voice. "Don't you think finding an open window is suspicious?"

Fiona's observation caught Sheldon off guard, but he quickly came up with a plausible explanation. "Sheldon wants to get you into the house. He wouldn't put obstacles in your way."

"No, I guess not." Exhaling, Fiona gathered up her cape and crawled over the windowsill.

Coop could feel the ghost's excitement as he followed her inside. After Sheldon closed and locked the window, Coop prepared to make his move.

The room was cast in shades of gray moonlight and dark shadow. Fiona stood in the middle with the fake talisman drooping from her hand.

"Shouldn't you begin?" Sheldon asked, infusing Coop's voice with distinctly amused arrogance.

"Yes, of course." Raising the chopstick, Fiona flipped the feathered charm back and forth as she walk around the empty space, intoning the nonsense spell.

> *Beneath this roof,*
> *Through haunted halls,*
> *Ghost be gone,*
> *Within these walls.*

Sheldon smiled with perverse pleasure as Fiona repeated the verse. He was enjoying the show, but his interest turned to impatience after a moment.

"There's no need to continue this charade, Fiona," Sheldon said. "It won't work."

"What?" Fiona stopped chanting. Her eyes narrowed with uncertainty.

"Foolish woman," Sheldon sneered. "You can't stop me."

The ghost apparently didn't think Coop could stop him either. Sheldon wasn't paying any attention to the other consciousness within the body he had possessed. *And that works to my advantage,* Coop thought.

"Sheldon?" Fiona gasped.

Coop concentrated his psychic energy to force the ghost's evacuation. His imagined phantom essence evaporated as his consciousness exploded from hiding. He felt the evil essence convulse, but the ghost didn't give. Empowered by revenge and a black soul that shunned surrender, Sheldon fought back. They pushed against each other, supernatural entities locked in a stalemate that held just long enough for Fiona to regain her wits. When she turned to run, Sheldon's rage drove Coop back down.

Horrified, Coop battered at the smothering presence, but the ghost's single-minded focus on killing Fiona was too strong to break. Sheldon caught the woman by the wrist and yanked her around.

"Get away from me!" Fiona struck him with the chopstick, creating a red welt on Coop's cheek.

The ghost was unfazed.

Coop pushed and pounded in a relentless attack to break the spirit's grip. He could not give up the struggle to save Fiona's life—or his own.

As Sheldon reached for Fiona's neck with Coop's hands, Fiona reached under her cape for the knife.

The sisters materialized between two mausoleums in the Nob Hill Gardens Cemetery. Backlit by the moon, the bare trees had a ghostly sheen that emphasized the gloomy ambience of the old graveyard. A musty odor clung to the gray stone crypts, and dry leaves crunched under the Charmed Ones' feet. There was a subtle stench of decay.

"Where's the main gate?" Phoebe peered through the moonlit darkness, looking for the rendezvous point Paige had arranged with Leo, Henry, and Victor.

"Sorry," Paige said. "I've never been here before, so I was orbing blind."

"Maybe they aren't here yet." Piper held the potion jar under her jacket.

"When I talked to Henry before we left the house, they were just driving up." Paige pulled her cell phone out of her sweatpants pocket.

"That was only a minute ago." Phoebe closed her eyes and empathically reached out. She thought she detected both resignation and purpose, but she couldn't pinpoint the location.

"No signal," Paige said, pocketing the phone.

"I'm not getting a signal either," Phoebe said. "So which way do we go?"

Piper panned her flashlight across a row of plain stone markers from the 1920s. The engraved names and dates were beginning to erode.

"Didn't Henry say anything about where to find Sheldon's grave?" Phoebe asked as she followed Piper. Fiona and Coop were in danger. Every minute mattered.

"It's in the middle," Paige replied. "On a path leading straight from the gate."

"That might help if we were by the gate." Piper paused to peer at a crumbling stone. "Wow, this grave has been here since 1872."

"So there's no logical layout by date that we can follow." Phoebe glanced at her watch. With little or no traffic, Coop and Fiona had probably arrived at the mansion by now. Jolted by a sudden, empathic influx of pain, she scanned for the source and picked up Victor's distress.

"That way." Picking up the pace, Phoebe led her sisters around recently dug mounds. Several yards on, they could hear the three men talking.

"Are we close?" Victor asked.

"It should be right around here somewhere," Henry said.

"Here's one from 1901," Leo said. "No, wait—the number's worn down." Phoebe, Piper, and Paige walked over as Leo squatted to wipe off the face of the stone. "This is it," he said. "'Sheldon Winters. Died May 19, 1907.'"

"Sorry we're late," Paige said. "I landed in the graveyard boonies and got us lost."

"Lost?" Victor leaned against a large stone, holding his shoe and rubbing his toes. "Is Phoebe's emotional sonar on the blink?"

"No," Phoebe said. "As soon as you stubbed your toe, I knew right where to find you." She glanced at Leo and Henry, who were still in partial costume. The seriousness of the circumstances overrode the comical aspects of Captain

Colonial and Robin Hood holding shovels in a cemetery. "What are you waiting for? Dig!"

Both men dug into the hard ground, but the effort had almost no effect.

"It's going to take hours to dig up this coffin," Leo said.

Phoebe and Prue had faced the same problem when they had attempted to dig up Elias Lundy. Prue had pulled the bones out of the ground with her telekinetic power. She couldn't help this time, but they had Paige.

"I don't know if I can orb something through all that dirt," Paige said.

"You orb things through air molecules," Leo explained, trying to bolster her confidence. "Dirt is just denser. That's the only difference."

"Try," Henry urged. "If it doesn't work, then we'll worry about what to do next."

"It'll work," Phoebe said. *It has to.*

Piper held the canning jar with her hand on the cap, ready to open and pour.

Coop braced for the agony of steel piercing his flesh. As much as Fiona loathed the idea of stabbing him, she had no choice. If she wanted to survive, she had to defend herself. He prayed the knife would miss arteries and vital organs so he'd have a fighting chance to live. Whitelighters couldn't heal wounds inflicted by a desperate, mortal woman.

"Get out of Coop now!" Fiona backed up her

fierce demand with a fistful of salt thrown in Coop's face.

The crystals stung Coop's eyes, but he was so surprised and relieved, he barely noticed. The blessed salt was devastating to the ghost.

Sheldon's sprit had easily eluded the toxic substance when Fiona threw it on his watery footprints. However, the ritual salt's properties were twenty times more potent when he was confined in a human body.

Coop immediately took advantage of Sheldon's diminished power to force him out. The enraged spirit fled, but battling the possession had weakened Coop. Gasping, he fell to his knees.

"Coop?" Fiona asked warily, still holding the knife.

"Yes." Aware that she might not—and should not—believe him without proof, Coop stayed still. Sheldon would not give up his prize without a fight.

Coop's eyes watered from the salt, making it hard to see, but now he had intimate knowledge of the ghost and knew what to expect. Anticipating Sheldon's next move, he sprang clear when a plasma ball rocketed toward him.

Fiona jumped aside too, but her evasive action was unnecessary. Sheldon did not want to end her life in flames. He wanted to choke her to death the same way he had killed his wife. But first, he wanted to make her suffer.

Sheldon slammed Fiona into the wall and snatched the knife from her hand. Moving faster than the human eye could track, the ghost slashed at the woman's face. She ducked, throwing up her arm to deflect the knife. The blade sliced her sleeve but didn't draw blood. Coop hadn't been able to move Fiona out of harm's way while Sheldon occupied his body. He had his powers back now, but he and Fiona still needed to keep the ghost distracted until the sisters completed the vanquishing ritual. He hoped they hurried. He couldn't wait much longer.

But Fiona wasn't helpless. She bolted across the room, shrugging out of her cape as she ran. When she reached the far wall, she whirled and folded the heavy cape to use as a shield.

"Protect your neck," Coop said as he dragged himself to his knees.

Fiona nodded and raised the cape up to her throat. Her gaze darted back and forth, searching for a flash of steel, ready to fend off another attack. "Where's the knife? If he cuts me—"

Coop knew what Fiona meant. If she were badly injured, she'd be too weak to resist. Their chances of holding Sheldon off until dawn, which was still a couple hours away, were already slim. But they had to delay only a short while longer.

"Only cowards torment women, Sheldon," Coop taunted.

The ghost answered with a barrage of plasma balls.

Coop ducked and dodged, but not fast enough. A flaming orb grazed his shoulder, burning his shirt and ear. Another singed his leg as he scrambled toward Fiona. Before he could reach her, Sheldon pinned her to the wall with a stream of blue lightning.

"Did you torture Victoria before you killed her?" Coop yelled as he struggled to stand. Once he was on his feet, he sprang into the line of fire. His body took the full force of Sheldon's plasma bolts.

Shielded from the attack, Fiona gasped and crumpled to the floor. Her collapse drew the ghost's attention.

Coop staggered as the blue bolts abruptly ended. He stayed upright, but the attack had drained more of his own energies. Swaying unsteadily, he watched in horror as the knife clutched in the ghost's invisible hand hovered over Fiona. "Look out!"

Although she was dazed and weakened, the ghost hunter rolled to the side as the blade descended. As the knife hit the wall, Sheldon's transparent form shimmered into view. The image flickered in and out like a strobe light several times before it stabilized.

Despite the ghost's dignified manner of dress—suit, high collar, vest, and tie—he exuded an aura of crazed evil. His black eyes glittered with hatred as he yanked the knife out of the wall and turned toward Fiona.

"Leave her alone!" Coop shouted, wondering if the spirit's visibility meant that Phoebe and her sisters had unearthed the grave.

Intent on the ghost hunter, Sheldon ignored him. As the ghost raised the knife to strike again, he flinched, then he frowned as though puzzled.

Coop held his breath. According to Phoebe, the ghost of Elias Lundy had felt every shovel strike when they were digging him up. The physical hits had alerted him to the danger and allowed him to hide his body. Lundy's body, however, had been buried quickly, under a tree, to hide the murder. Sheldon had had a proper funeral and was buried in a coffin. That would minimize the effects of being exhumed. Still, even though the sisters would take care not to repeat their mistake, they couldn't avoid disturbing his bones a little.

While Sheldon hesitated, Fiona slowly moved backward. Suddenly, the ghost dropped the knife and lunged. Sheldon ripped the cape out of her hands and grabbed her around the neck.

Coop flung himself at the ghost, but he passed right through the apparition and sprawled on the floor. Sheldon had physical capabilities he couldn't counteract.

Gagging, Fiona tried to pry the ghostly

fingers off her throat. All she clutched was air, but she didn't stop fighting. When her eyes suddenly widened, Coop tried to dislodge the ghost again. As he started to push himself between Fiona and the ghost, he saw a black spot appear on the floor between Sheldon's feet.

The ghost didn't notice the dark speck immediately. Coop couldn't be sure the gates of hell were opening to consume Sheldon Winters' malicious soul, but *some*thing was happening. He closed his arms around Fiona's waist. The instant Sheldon loosened his hold, Coop pulled Fiona back.

Coughing, Fiona pressed against Coop. Her gaze, like his, was fastened on the ghost.

Sheldon glanced around with an annoyed look, as if a pesky fly were buzzing him. His expression shifted from perplexed uncertainty to stunned terror as a fiery circle opened underneath him. "No!" Realizing the horror of his imminent fate, he screamed and tried to move away, but his essence was trapped. As the fire moved up his legs and torso to fully envelop him, Sheldon's cruel face contorted with pain. His shrieks of outrage and fear reverberated in the empty room as his essence was pulled down into the blazing maw. The opening closed, leaving no trace of the ghost behind, only silence.

"Is he gone?" Fiona asked in a rasping voice.

"I think it's safe to say that's the last we'll ever see of Sheldon Winters." Coop rose and dusted off his jeans and checkered shirt. Then he offered Fiona his hand.

Fiona picked up the kitchen knife Sheldon had dropped and smiled as Coop helped her up. "Yep. I think so."

Chapter Twelve

Coop and Fiona walked into the Manor just as Piper finished emptying the dishwasher. She rinsed the canning jar with soapy water and set it in the top rack. "It's about time you two got here," she teased.

"We didn't take the magical express," Coop said.

"Coop wanted to drive," Fiona confessed.

"And you let him?" Phoebe gasped.

Fiona shrugged. "He didn't hit anything."

"Good thing for him," O'Brien said. "It's a lot of bad luck Coop would be havin' if anything happened to you, Fiona."

"Coop saved my life, O'Brien." Fiona turned to Paige. "He needs some of your magic medicine."

"You're hurt?" Phoebe ran to her husband and examined the wounds on his shoulder and ear.

"Just a flesh wound, ma'am," Coop joked, back in cowboy mode.

Rolling her eyes, Paige eased Phoebe aside. "Make room for Paige, *pardner*."

"I am so glad to see you!" Phoebe told Fiona.

"And I am so glad to be here!" Grinning, Fiona handed the kitchen knife back to Piper, then flicked the chopstick talisman back and forth. "Would you mind if I kept this as a souvenir?"

"It's yours!" Piper set a stack of dirty dishes in the sink to soak.

Victor walked in through the hall door. "What smells so good?"

"Late-night breakfast," Piper said. "Are the kids asleep?"

"Finally," Victor said. "If we could bottle kid go-power, we wouldn't have an energy crisis."

"The darlin' lads were no trouble to us a'tall," Seamus said. He and the other leprechauns were seated around the table.

Victor poured a cup of freshly brewed coffee and sat down. "What did you guys do with Wyatt and Chris while we were gone?"

"Grady played a pennywhistle lullaby, and the lads nodded right off," Seamus said. "*You* woke them up to bring them back here."

"Because we didn't want Wyatt orbing home in the morning to get his Halloween candy," Leo explained as he came in. His hair was damp after a quick cleanup, and he had changed into jeans and a T-shirt.

"At least my wife will be able to orb after

them," Henry said, kissing Paige on the cheek. He had also changed back into regular clothes.

"If they *can* orb," Paige mused. "Our kids will only be one-quarter Whitelighter."

"Nobody's had to worry about that before," Leo said. "But I'm guessing the magical side of the family is dominant."

"I never thought I'd say this, but I hope you're right." Henry slid into a chair and reached for a piece of coffee cake. "How did this survive the demolition?"

"It was frozen." Piper started cracking eggs for cheese and onion omelets. Cooking took her mind off the clutter she couldn't take care of until the dishwasher finished another cycle.

"Where's Ken?" Fiona asked.

"Oh, he left as soon as he came to." O'Brien winked at her. "He said he wouldn't be givin' you the satisfaction of ever mentioning what happened here. And he won't write about it, either."

"Now, that's a stroke of luck," Phoebe said.

Piper noticed the leprechauns' guilty and amused reactions. "I don't suppose you guys had anything to do with that."

"A favor for O'Brien, it was," Liam said, "for asking Paige to bring us back to celebrate Samhain." He raised his glass of cider in salute to his friend.

"And a wonderful Samhain we had, too."

Grady grinned. "Even crusty old Connor had a splendid time of it."

"Bah." Connor stuffed a cookie in his mouth so he wouldn't smile.

"Well, I'm glad you all had fun." Paige cocked her head. "You didn't get into any trouble, did you?"

"None that you'll be hearin' about," Seamus assured her.

"Except for runnin' 'round the neighborhood in the wandering pants, looking for the laddie that was callin' the knickers home," Liam said.

"Pants?" Piper stopped whisking the eggs. "Wyatt's soldier sweats?"

Leo nodded. "Wyatt cast a word spell to make the pants come back."

"And it worked?" Piper beamed with pride. "That's our boy."

"Well, it's almost dawn and time for us to be goin'," Grady said. "We'll take the dead lads back with us on the Rainbow Road. Then they can bid a proper farewell to all their old friends."

"But don't fret, Paige." Liam patted her hand. "We'll be back in the otherworld before the portal closes at dawn."

"So . . ." Paige hesitated, her look questioning. "Does that mean all is forgiven?"

"Aye, and more," O'Brien admitted sheepishly. "We were wrong to hold a grudge against you when a hex was to blame."

"But we're mighty grateful for the best

Samhain ever," Marty said, "even with no mutton or bonfire."

"Farewell, Fiona." O'Brien tipped his hat as the rainbow appeared. "Until we meet again."

"Happy trails!" Phoebe waved as the leprechauns and their colorful road disappeared.

"Well, I guess I'd better be going too." Fiona started to rise.

Coop pulled her back down. "Not before you have something to eat. You must be hungry after your grand adventure."

"Now that it's over, I can honestly say . . . it *was* rather grand, wasn't it?" Fiona settled back in her seat and tucked the talisman into her cape. "But I do have a favor to ask."

"We're listening." Piper smiled as she passed out paper plates and plastic silverware.

"I'd like to write an article about the ghosts of Sheldon and Victoria Winters," Fiona said. "From the original murder and suicide to my unwitting role in the tragedy and Sheldon's fiery end."

"It's a great story," Phoebe said. "Victoria is saved from a miserable afterlife. Sheldon is doomed to spend eternity in hell, and justice is served. I'd want to write it too."

"But we can't be in it," Paige cautioned.

"Not a problem," Fiona said. "As long as you don't want credit for what happened, I can tell the story without any references to you or the Manor."

"The one thing we don't want is credit," Paige said.

"But what if Ken changes his mind and decides to set the record straight?" Piper gave Fiona the first omelet.

"The last thing *Ken* wants is to give credence to anything I say," Fiona said. "He knows that what happened here was real, but he would never admit it, and he certainly wouldn't go public with it."

"Then permission granted." Piper set another omelet in front of Leo, then paused. "I owe you an apology."

"For what?" Leo bit into a piece of toast.

"For not listening when you warned me that evil was still out there, waiting to strike when we least expected it," Piper said. "I'll be more wary from now on."

"Thank you." Leo slipped his arm around her waist and squeezed her affectionately.

"I need to apologize too," Phoebe said, "for not telling anyone about my vision. I promise I won't do that again, no matter how disturbing the images are."

"Good." Piper sighed. "Obviously, as serene and secure as our lives might seem now, there are still bad guys out there, and we're still the Charmed Ones."

"And you won't always have an evil-of-the-day expert on hand to help out." Leo smiled at the ghost hunter.

"You flatter me." Fiona took a bite of omelet and nodded her approval. "Delicious."

"Thanks!" Piper smiled, genuinely pleased. "I've been toying with the idea of selling my nightclub and opening a restaurant. It just seems like the right thing to do."

"Which reminds me." Paige set down her teacup and folded her arms. "Our haunted Halloween might not have ended so happily if we hadn't had the ghost-vanquishing information in the Book of Shadows."

"That book has saved the day more than once," Victor agreed.

"Yes, but the spell alone wasn't enough to stop Elias Lundy," Paige went on. "The lessons Piper and Phoebe learned from their mistakes with Lundy and Fiona's knowledge of what makes ghosts tick made Sheldon's vanquish possible."

"That's true." Piper poured another batch of omelet mix into the frying pan. "I assume you have a point."

"Yes, I do." Paige sat back. "We're going to have a bunch of kids and grandkids, and so will other magical people. Those new generations will need all the help they can get. So I'm going to collect all the information I can about everything a witch or a Whitelighter might need to know."

"We need a book like that in Magic School library," Leo said.

"Exactly, and I want to start with ghosts." Paige glanced at Fiona. "If you'll let me pick your brain."

"I'd be thrilled to help any way I can," Fiona said. "On one condition."

"What?" the Charmed Ones asked in unison.

"Please invite me to your Halloween party next year!"

"You have a standing invitation, Fiona," Phoebe said. "Although, I'm afraid the neighbors will be disappointed when next year's open house isn't nearly as exciting."

"I can fix that," Paige said. Her eyes twinkled like a leprechaun's as she teased, "I'll just open a portal to the otherworld so the spirits can come through for Samhain."

"No!" everyone shouted.

About the Author

Diana G. Gallagher lives in Florida with her husband, Marty Burke, five dogs, four cats, and a cranky parrot. Her hobbies are gardening, garage sales, and her grandchildren. Although she aspired to write from age twelve, she has been an English equitation instructor, a professional folk musician, and an artist.

While writing *The Alien Dark* (TSR, 1990), her first published novel, Gallagher also tried her hand at whimsical fantasy art. Best known for her hand-colored prints depicting Woof: The House Dragon, she won a Hugo for Best Fan Artist 1988.

Gallagher has written for young and middle readers, teens, and adults in several series: *Buffy the Vampire Slayer*, *Charmed*, *Smallville*, *Sabrina the Teenage Witch*, *The Secret World of Alex Mack*, and *Star Trek*, among others. She is a coauthor of *No Ordinary Heroes*, of a nonfiction account of events at the Orleans Parish Jail during Hurricane Katrina.

Charmed

"We're the protectors of the innocent.
We're known as the Charmed Ones."

–Phoebe Halliwell, "Something Wicca This Way Comes"

Go behind the scenes of television's sexiest supernatural thriller with *The Book of Three*, the *only* fully authorized companion to the witty, witchy world of *Charmed*!

Official **Charmed** Web Store

Visit www.seenoncharmed.com for exclusive
merchandise and items SeenON! Charmed season 7.

seen
ON!

SHOP
seenoncharmed.com

**Girls searching for answers . . .
and finding themselves.**